Arne Herold

Type 2 Diabetes
Food Guide

Introduction

This book provides a comprehensive overview of different foods and their effects on blood sugar levels, specifically targeted at people with type 2 diabetes. It provides detailed information about the glycemic index (GI) and glycemic load (GL) of various foods, as well as their nutrient profiles, including carbohydrate content, fiber, protein, and fats. The focus is on how these nutrients work together to regulate blood sugar levels and support a balanced, healthy diet.

The goal of this book is to provide people with type 2 diabetes with a helpful and easy-to-understand resource to help them make conscious and healthy choices about their diet. The selection of foods has been carefully made to offer a variety of healthy, nutritious options that keep blood sugar levels stable while not neglecting enjoyment and taste.

It's important to emphasize that everyone's body reacts differently to food, and the information presented in this book provides general guidelines. Individual nutritional advice with a doctor or nutritionist remains indispensable in order to optimally meet personal health goals and nutritional needs.

I hope that you will enjoy this book.

The satisfaction of my readers is particularly important to me, and I would be very happy if you could send me your feedback on the book.

I would like to ask you to take a moment to write a customer review on Amazon. In this way, you support other readers in making purchasing decisions and contribute to constantly improving my offer.

Thank you very much!

Arne Herold

Content

Acai Berries

Glycemic Index (GI): 12 (low)

Carbohydrate content: 4 g per 100 g

Fibre content: 2 g per 100 g

Protein: 2 g per 100 g

Fat content: 5 g per 100 g

Serving Size: 1/2 cup frozen or mashed (about 100 g)

Glycemic load (GL): Very low

Special Benefits: Acai berries are rich in antioxidants, especially anthocyanins, which have anti-inflammatory properties and may contribute to heart health. They provide a good source of healthy fats such as omega-6 and omega-9 and contain important micronutrients such as vitamin A, calcium and iron.

Recommended Preparation Methods: Acai berries can be used as frozen fruits, puree, or powder. They are ideal for smoothie bowls, yoghurt mixes or as an ingredient in mueslis and desserts.

Acerola

Glycemic Index (GI): Low

Carbohydrate content: 8 g per 100 g

Fiber content: 1.1 g per 100 g

Protein: 0.4 g per 100 g

Fat content: 0.3 g per 100 g

Serving Size: 1 cup (about 100 g)

Glycemic load (GL): Very low

Special benefits: Acerola is particularly rich in vitamin C, which strengthens the immune system and has antioxidant properties. It also contains vitamin A and various B vitamins. The antioxidants found in acerola can reduce inflammation and contribute to overall health. In addition, it is low in calories and offers fiber, which can have a positive effect on digestion.

Recommended preparation methods: Fresh as an addition to smoothies or juices, in salads or as a natural sweetener in desserts and yogurt. Acerola can also be used as a powder in various recipes to increase vitamin C content.

Alfalfa sprouts

Glycemic Index (GI): Unknown, but very low due to the minimal carbohydrate content

Carbohydrate content: 2.1 g per 100 g

Fiber content: 1.9 g per 100 g

Protein: 3.9 g per 100 g

Fat content: 0.2 g per 100 g

Serving Size: One handful (approx. 30 g)

Glycemic load (GL): Very low

Special benefits: Alfalfa sprouts are an excellent source of vitamins such as vitamin K, vitamin C, and vitamin A. They also contain a variety of minerals, including calcium, magnesium, and iron. Their nutrient density makes them an excellent food for diabetics, as they can help keep blood sugar levels stable. In addition, alfalfa sprouts are rich in antioxidants and contain botanicals that could have anti-inflammatory properties.

Recommended Preparation Methods: Alfalfa sprouts can be used raw in salads, sandwiches, or wraps. They are also a popular ingredient for smoothies or can serve as a garnish on soups and other dishes. It is important to wash alfalfa sprouts thoroughly to avoid possible contamination.

Almond flour

Glycemic Index (GI): 5 (very low)

Carbohydrate content: 20 g per 100 g

Fiber content: 12 g per 100 g

Protein: 24 g per 100 g

Fat content: 52 g per 100 g

Serving Size: 1/4 cup (about 28 g)

Glycemic load (GL): Very low

Special advantages:

- Almond flour is very low in carbohydrates and high in fiber, which makes it particularly suitable for type 2 diabetics.

- It contains a high amount of healthy unsaturated fatty acids, which can help lower cholesterol levels.

- Vitamin E and magnesium are abundant in almond flour, both important for heart health and blood sugar regulation.

- Almond flour is gluten-free, making it an excellent alternative for people with celiac disease or gluten intolerance.

Recommended preparation methods:

- As a substitute for wheat flour in baking recipes, such as bread, muffins or biscuits.

- For thickening sauces or soups.

- In smoothies or yogurt for extra nutritional content.

- As a breading for meat or vegetables, for example when baking or frying.

Almond milk (unsweetened)

Glycemic Index (GI): 30 (low)

Carbohydrate content: 0.6 g per 100 ml

Fiber content: 0.1 g per 100 ml

Protein: 0.5 g per 100 ml

Fat content: 3.6 g per 100 ml

Serving Size: 1 cup (about 240 ml)

Glycemic load (GL): Very low

Special advantages:

- Low in calories and contains minimal amounts of carbohydrates, making it an excellent milk alternative for diabetics.

- Good source of vitamin E, a powerful antioxidant that can help protect cell membranes.

- Often enriched with additional vitamins and minerals such as calcium and vitamin D to improve nutrient absorption.

Recommended preparation methods:

- Directly as a drink or as an ingredient in various recipes such as smoothies, coffee, tea or baked goods.

- Can also be used as a base for sauces, dressings or soups.

Note: Be sure to choose unsweetened variants to avoid extra sugar and calories.

Almonds

Glycemic Index (GI): 0 (low)

Carbohydrate content: 22 g per 100 g

Fiber content: 12.5 g per 100 g

Protein: 21 g per 100 g

Fat content: 50 g per 100 g

Serving Size: 1 ounce (about 28 g)

Glycemic load (GL): Very low

Special benefits: Almonds are an excellent choice for people with type 2 diabetes because they have a very low glycemic index and minimal glycemic load. They are rich in healthy unsaturated fats, fiber, and protein, which can help stabilize blood sugar levels. Almonds also contain important nutrients such as vitamin E, magnesium and antioxidants, which have anti-inflammatory effects and can promote heart health. The high fiber content also aids digestion and can help with weight management, which is often a part of diabetes management.

Recommended preparation methods: Almonds can be used in many ways. They can be enjoyed raw as a snack, roasted or as an ingredient in various dishes such as salads, yogurt, smoothies or baked goods. Almond butter and almond milk are also popular alternatives. However, with roasted almonds, attention should be paid to the salt content, as too much salt can have negative effects on blood pressure.

Amaranth

Glycemic Index (GI): 35–50 (low to medium)

Carbohydrate content: 19 g per 100 g

Fiber content: 6 g per 100 g

Protein: 9 g per 100 g

Fat content: 1.8 g per 100 g

Serving Size: 1 cup cooked (about 246 g)

Glycemic Load (GL): Low to Medium

Special advantages:

Amaranth is an excellent source of vegetable protein and contains all nine essential amino acids, making it a complete source of protein.

It is rich in fiber, which can promote digestive health and increase satiety.

Amaranth contains important micronutrients such as magnesium, iron, calcium, and phosphorus, which are important for bone health and other bodily functions.

It's also rich in antioxidants, which can help reduce cell damage caused by free radicals and fight inflammation.

Recommended preparation methods:

- Cooked and as an accompaniment to main courses.

- In salads as a topping for extra crunch and nutrients.
- As an ingredient in baked goods such as bread and muffins for extra nutritional content.
- Porridge-like as a nutritious breakfast, often cooked and served with milk or plant-based milk, as well as fruits and nuts.

Amaranth is a versatile and nutrient-dense choice that meets the needs of diabetics while providing many health benefits.

Anchovy

Glycemic Index (GI): 0 (not applicable as there are almost no carbohydrates)

Carbohydrate content: 0 g per 100 g

Fiber content: 0 g per 100 g

Protein: 20 g per 100 g

Fat content: 10 g per 100 g

Serving Size: 1 can (approx. 30 g)

Glycemic Load (GL): Not applicable

Special benefits: Anchovies are an excellent source of high-quality protein and rich in omega-3 fatty acids, which is good for heart health. They also contain beneficial micronutrients such as calcium, iron, and vitamin D. Omega-3 fatty acids can reduce inflammation and are associated with improved insulin sensitivity, which may be beneficial for diabetics.

Recommended preparation methods: Directly from the can as a snack, in salads, on pizza or as a condiment in sauces and dressings.

Anchovies are a good choice for people with type 2 diabetes due to their high protein and omega-3 fatty acid content, as well as their low carbohydrate content.

Apples

Glycemic Index (GI): 39 (low)

Carbohydrate content: 14 g per 100 g

Fibre content: 2.4 g per 100 g

Protein: 0.3 g per 100 g

Fat content: 0.2 g per 100 g

Serving Size: 1 medium apple (approx. 182 g)

Glycemic Load (GL): Low

Special benefits: Apples are rich in fiber, especially pectin, which helps control blood sugar. They offer a variety of vitamins such as vitamin C and a good amount of antioxidants that can reduce oxidative damage. Eating apples can also help protect the cardiovascular system and promote overall health.

Recommended Preparation Methods: Apples can be eaten raw, cut into salads, made into applesauce, baked, or used as an ingredient in various healthy recipes.

Apricots

Glycemic Index (GI): 34 (low)

Carbohydrate content: 11.1 g per 100 g

Fibre content: 2 g per 100 g

Protein: 0.5 g per 100 g

Fat content: 0.1 g per 100 g

Serving Size: 4 fresh apricots (approx. 70 g)

Glycemic Load (GL): Low

Special benefits: Apricots are rich in vitamins C and A, which are important for immune function and vision. They also contain antioxidants such as beta-carotene and flavonoids, which can help reduce cell damage and fight inflammation. Apricots are also a good source of fiber, which can aid digestion and help stabilize blood sugar levels.

Recommended preparation methods: Fresh as a snack, in salads, or in yoghurt and muesli. They can also be dried or used as an ingredient in savory and sweet dishes. However, with dried apricots, attention should be paid to the sugar content.

Artichokes

Glycemic Index (GI): 20 (low)

Carbohydrate content: 11 g per 100 g

Fibre content: 5.4 g per 100 g

Protein: 3.3 g per 100 g

Fat content: 0.2 g per 100 g

Serving Size: 1 medium artichoke (approx. 120 g)

Glycemic load (GL): Very low

Special advantages:

- Promotes digestion and helps regulate blood sugar levels.

- Rich in antioxidants: Contains compounds like silymarin and quercetin that can help fight cell damage caused by free radicals.

- High content of vitamins and minerals: Especially rich in folic acid, vitamin C, vitamin K, and magnesium.

Recommended preparation methods:

- Steaming: Preserves most of the nutrients and preserves the natural flavor.

- Cooking: Works well for making artichoke hearts, which can be used in various recipes.

- Grilling: Gives the artichokes a smoky, intense flavor.

Tip: Artichokes can be served as a main course or as a side dish. The leaves dip well into dips, and the hearts can be added to salads, soups, or pasta dishes.

Asparagus

Glycemic Index (GI): 15 (low)

Carbohydrate content: 3.9 g per 100 g

Fiber content: 2.1 g per 100 g

Protein: 2.2 g per 100 g

Fat content: 0.1 g per 100 g

Serving Size: 1 cup cooked (about 134 g)

Glycemic load (GL): Very low

Special advantages: Asparagus is rich in fiber, vitamins A, C, E and K as well as folic acid. It also contains valuable antioxidants that can reduce oxidative stress. The high water content supports hydration, and asparagus has anti-inflammatory properties that promote overall health.

Recommended preparation methods: steaming, grilling, roasting or raw in salads.

Avocado

Glycemic Index (GI): 15 (low)

Carbohydrate content: 9 g per 100 g

Fibre content: 7 g per 100 g

Protein: 2 g per 100 g

Fat content: 15 g per 100 g (mostly healthy monounsaturated fatty acids)

Serving Size: 1/2 avocado (approx. 100 g)

Glycemic load (GL): Very low

Special benefits: Avocado is rich in healthy fats, especially monounsaturated fatty acids, which can support the cardiovascular system. It also contains high amounts of fiber, which can aid digestion and stabilize blood sugar levels. Avocado also provides a good source of vitamins and minerals such as vitamin K, vitamin E, vitamin C, B vitamins and potassium. Antioxidants in avocado can help reduce inflammation and support overall cellular health.

Recommended preparation methods: Consume raw, as a spread (guacamole), in salads, as an addition to smoothies or as a topping on various dishes. Avoid using avocado in highly processed forms that may contain additional unhealthy fats or sugars.

Avocado oil

Glycemic Index (GI): 0 (very low as it does not contain carbohydrates)

Carbohydrate content: 0 g per 100 g

Fiber content: 0 g per 100 g

Protein: 0 g per 100 g

Fat content: 100 g per 100 g

Serving Size: 1 tablespoon (about 14 g)

Glycemic load (GL): Very low

Special advantages:

Avocado oil is rich in monounsaturated fatty acids, which can help improve cardiovascular health. It also contains a high amount of vitamin E and antioxidant compounds such as lutein, which can act as anti-inflammatory.

Recommended preparation methods:

Avocado oil is great for frying, grilling, and baking because it has a high smoke point. It can also be used raw as a dressing for salads or as an ingredient in dips and sauces.

Bamboo shoots

Glycemic Index (GI): 20 (low)

Carbohydrate content: 5.2 g per 100 g

Fiber content: 2.2 g per 100 g

Protein: 2.6 g per 100 g

Fat content: 0.3 g per 100 g

Serving Size: 1 cup cooked (about 120 g)

Glycemic load (GL): Very low

Special benefits: Bamboo shoots are low in calories and high in fiber, which can help maintain stable blood sugar levels. They also contain valuable minerals such as potassium and phosphorus and phytochemicals that have antioxidant and anti-inflammatory properties.

Recommended preparation methods: boiling, steaming, in soups and stews or as an ingredient in salads and stir-fries.

Bamboo shoots are an excellent choice for people with type 2 diabetes because they help control blood sugar and provide a variety of nutrients. The preparation is varied and makes it possible to take advantage of its nutritional benefits in a varied diet.

Banana (in moderation)

Glycemic Index (GI): 51 (medium)

Carbohydrate content: 22.8 g per 100 g

Fibre content: 2.6 g per 100 g

Protein: 1.1 g per 100 g

Fat content: 0.3 g per 100 g

Serving Size: 1 small banana (approx. 100 g)

Glycemic load (GL): Medium

Special benefits: Bananas are an excellent source of potassium, vitamin C, and vitamin B6. They help regulate blood pressure and are good for the heart. Bananas also contain short-chain carbohydrates, which can quickly raise blood sugar levels, which is especially important for diabetics. The fiber found in bananas, such as pectin, helps regulate blood sugar levels.

Recommended preparation methods: Eat raw, in smoothies or as a side dish in fruit salads. However, due to their natural sugar content, diabetics should moderate the consumption of bananas and ideally consume them together with high-fiber or protein-rich foods to avoid a sharp rise in blood sugar.

Barley

Glycemic Index (GI): 25 (low)

Carbohydrate content: 28 g per 100 g

Fiber content: 17.3 g per 100 g

Protein: 2.3 g per 100 g

Fat content: 2.1 g per 100 g

Serving Size: 1 cup cooked (about 157 g)

Glycemic Load (GL): Low

Special benefits: Barley is rich in soluble and insoluble fiber, which promotes digestion and prolongs satiety. It also contains important minerals such as magnesium, manganese, and selenium, as well as B vitamins, which can help maintain a healthy metabolism. The high fiber content of beta-glucan can help regulate blood sugar levels and lower LDL cholesterol.

Recommended ways of preparation: Barley can be used as an accompaniment to main courses, in soups and stews, as an ingredient in salads or as a base for breakfast porridge. Boiling or pressure cooking are common preparation methods.

Barley is an excellent choice for type 2 diabetics due to its low glycemic index and high fiber levels, and can help keep blood sugar levels stable throughout the day.

Basil

Glycemic Index (GI): Not applicable (low to negligible)

Carbohydrate content: 3 g per 100 g

Fibre content: 1.6 g per 100 g

Protein: 3.2 g per 100 g

Fat content: 0.6 g per 100 g

Serving Size: 1 tablespoon chopped (about 2.5 g)

Glycemic load (GL): Very low

Special advantages:

- Rich in vitamin K, vitamin A and vitamin C.

- Contains essential oils such as eugenol, which have anti-inflammatory properties.

- Has antibacterial and antioxidant properties that can reduce cell damage.

- May promote digestion and reduce bloating.

Recommended preparation methods:

- Fresh as a garnish for salads, soups or sandwiches.

- As an ingredient in pestos or dressings.

- Dried or fresh to enhance pasta, sauces and other dishes.

Beans (black, white, red)

Glycemic Index (GI): Black: 30 (low), White: 35 (low), Red: 40 (low)

Carbohydrate content: 21 g per 100 g

Fibre content: 7 g per 100 g

Protein: 8 g per 100 g

Fat content: 0.5 g per 100 g

Serving Size: 1/2 cup cooked (about 130 g)

Glycemic Load (GL): Low

Special advantages:

- Rich in fiber: Helps control blood sugar and promotes satiety.
- **Protein:** Supports muscle building and repair.
- Source of important minerals: Contains iron, magnesium and potassium, which are necessary for various bodily functions.
- Antioxidants: May reduce inflammation and protect cells from damage.
- Heart Healthy: May lower cholesterol levels, thus reducing the risk of heart disease.

Recommended preparation methods:

- **Stews and soups**: Perfect for hearty and nutritious dishes.
- **Salads**: Beans can be used both cold and warm in salads.

- **Dipping and spreading**: Pureed as a spread or dip, for example in hummus variations.
- **Legume salads**

Beans are an excellent addition to the diet of type 2 diabetics, as they promote a slow release of glucose and thus help with better blood sugar control.

Beans (green)

Glycemic Index (GI): 15 (low)

Carbohydrate content: 7 g per 100 g

Fiber content: 3.4 g per 100 g

Protein: 1.8 g per 100 g

Fat content: 0.1 g per 100 g

Serving Size: 1 cup cooked (about 125 g)

Glycemic load (GL): Very low

Special benefits: Green beans are an excellent source of fiber, which can help stabilize blood sugar levels. They are rich in vitamins such as vitamins K, C and A, as well as various important minerals such as folic acid and magnesium. The antioxidants it contains can reduce inflammation in the body and may offer protection against chronic diseases.

Recommended preparation methods: Steam, boil or lightly sauté. Green beans can also be used raw and fresh in salads.

Beef steak (lean)

Glycemic Index (GI): 0 (very low)

Carbohydrate content: 0 g per 100 g

Fiber content: 0 g per 100 g

Protein: 31 g per 100 g

Fat content: 3.5 g per 100 g

Serving Size: 1 serving (approx. 150 g)

Glycemic load (GL): Very low

Special advantages:

- Rich in high-quality protein, which is important for muscle building and maintaining muscle mass.

- Low carbohydrate content, which contributes to more stable blood sugar levels.

- Contains essential amino acids and vitamins such as vitamins B12, B6 as well as minerals such as iron and zinc, which are important for blood formation and the immune system.

Recommended preparation methods:

- Grill or roast at low to medium temperature to avoid the formation of unhealthy trans fats.

- Sauté briefly and sharply, then finish cooking at a low temperature to keep it tender and juicy.

- Use healthy fats for frying, such as olive oil or avocado oil, to increase nutritional value.

Beef steak can be an excellent source of protein for type 2 diabetics when consumed lean and in moderate amounts. It should preferably be consumed in combination with high-fiber vegetables to ensure a balanced meal.

Beetroot

Glycemic Index (GI): 64 (medium)

Carbohydrate content: 10 g per 100 g

Fiber content: 2.8 g per 100 g

Protein: 1.6 g per 100 g

Fat content: 0.2 g per 100 g

Serving Size: 1 cup cooked (about 170 g)

Glycemic load (GL): Medium

Special advantages:

- Rich in fiber, which can help regulate blood sugar levels.

- Contains betaine, which has anti-inflammatory properties.

- High content of folic acid, which is important for heart health.

- Good source of antioxidants such as betalain, which can protect cells from damage.

-

Recommended preparation methods:

- Steaming, boiling or roasting.

- Can be used raw in salads.

- Also popular as a juice or in smoothies.

Despite its medium glycemic index, beetroot offers numerous health benefits and can be a part of a balanced diet for people with type 2 diabetes in moderation.

Berry mix

Glycemic Index (GI): 25-40 (depending on the type of berry, usually low)

Carbohydrate content: 14 g per 100 g

Fiber content: 5 g per 100 g

Protein: 1 g per 100 g

Fat content: 0.3 g per 100 g

Serving Size: 1 cup (about 150 g)

Glycemic Load (GL): Low

Special benefits: Berries are rich in fiber, vitamins (especially vitamins C and K), minerals and antioxidants. They have anti-inflammatory properties and can help stabilize blood sugar levels. They also contain anthocyanins, which promote heart health.

Recommended preparation methods: Excellent in smoothies, yogurt, oatmeal, salads or as a snack. Berries can also be frozen and used later without losing their valuable nutrients.

Black beans

Glycemic Index (GI): 30 (low)

Carbohydrate content: 63 g per 100 g (uncooked)

Fibre content: 15 g per 100 g (uncooked)

Protein: 21 g per 100 g (uncooked)

Fat content: 0.9 g per 100 g (uncooked)

Serving Size: 1/2 cup cooked (about 85 g)

Glycemic Load (GL): Low

Special benefits: Rich in fiber and protein, contains antioxidants such as polyphenols, promotes stable blood sugar control and improves digestive health.

Recommended ways to prepare: Boil, add to soup or stew, use as a side dish or ingredient in salads.

Black beans are especially beneficial for type 2 diabetics because they have a low glycemic index and are high in fiber, which helps keep blood sugar levels stable. They are also a good source of plant-based protein and support digestive health thanks to their high fiber content. The antioxidants in black beans help reduce inflammation and lower the risk of chronic disease.

Blackberries

Glycemic Index (GI): 25 (low)

Carbohydrate content: 10 g per 100 g

Fibre content: 5.3 g per 100 g

Protein: 1.4 g per 100 g

Fat content: 0.5 g per 100 g

Serving Size: 1 cup (about 140 g)

Glycemic load (GL): Very low

Special benefits: Blackberries are rich in fiber, which helps regulate blood sugar levels and promotes digestion. They are an excellent source of vitamins C and K and contain a good amount of manganese. Antioxidants in blackberries, such as anthocyanins, promote cardiovascular health and can have anti-inflammatory effects. In addition, they provide few calories and have a natural, sweet taste that can prevent cravings for sweets.

Recommended preparation methods: They can be used fresh as a snack, mixed into yogurt, integrated into smoothies, used as a topping for cereals or salads, or made into sugar-free jellies and jams. Baking in muffins or cakes is also possible, although sugar substitutes can be used to keep blood sugar levels better under control.

Blackcurrants

Glycemic Index (GI): 15 (low)

Carbohydrate content: 6 g per 100 g

Fiber content: 5 g per 100 g

Protein: 1.4 g per 100 g

Fat content: 0.2 g per 100 g

Serving Size: 1 cup (about 150 g)

Glycemic load (GL): Very low

Special benefits: Blackcurrants are an excellent source of vitamin C and contain high amounts of anthocyanins, which are potent antioxidants. These antioxidants can help lower the risk of cardiovascular disease and reduce inflammatory processes in the body. In addition, the fiber in blackcurrants can help regulate blood sugar levels, making it an excellent choice for people with type 2 diabetes.

Recommended Preparation Methods: Blackcurrants can be consumed fresh, mixed into smoothies or added to yogurt. They can also be made into sauces or used as a base for low-sugar compotes and jams.

Blueberries

Glycemic Index (GI): 53 (medium)

Carbohydrate content: 14.5 g per 100 g

Fibre content: 2.4 g per 100 g

Protein: 0.7 g per 100 g

Fat content: 0.3 g per 100 g

Serving Size: 1 cup (about 150 g)

Glycemic load (GL): Medium

Special benefits: Blueberries are rich in fiber, antioxidants (mainly anthocyanins), and vitamin C. These nutrients can help reduce inflammation and improve insulin sensitivity.

Recommended preparation methods: Fresh as a snack, in smoothies, over yoghurt or oatmeal, in salads, as a topping for desserts or slightly warmed as a fruit compote.

Borage

Glycemic Index (GI): N/A (very low, exact values not often given)

Carbohydrate content: Very low (approx. 3 g per 100 g)

Fibre content: Moderate (approx. 1 g per 100 g)

Protein: 1.8 g per 100 g

Fat content: 0.7 g per 100 g

Serving Size: 1 cup chopped (about 21 g)

Glycemic load (GL): Very low

Special benefits: Borage is rich in gamma-linolenic acid (a type of omega-6 fatty acid), which can have anti-inflammatory effects. It also contains vitamin C, magnesium and iron. The leaves and flowers can also be used as an aromatic spice and traditionally have calming and mood-balancing properties.

Recommended preparation methods: Borage leaves and flowers can be used fresh in salads, smoothies or as a garnish. The leaves can also be boiled or steamed and served as a vegetable side dish. In Mediterranean cuisine, borage is often added to soups and stews.

Brown rice

Glycemic Index (GI): 50 (medium)

Carbohydrate content: 23 g per 100 g

Fiber content: 1.8 g per 100 g

Protein: 2.6 g per 100 g

Fat content: 0.9 g per 100 g

Serving Size: 1/2 cup cooked (about 100 g)

Glycemic load (GL): Medium

Special Benefits: Brown rice is a good source of fiber, magnesium, and selenium, which can be helpful for heart health and metabolism. It also contains antioxidants and phytonutrients that can boost the immune system.

Recommended ways to prepare: Cooked as a side dish, in salads, or as a base for dishes such as stir-fry and rice stir-fries.

Brussels sprouts

Glycemic Index (GI): 15 (low)

Carbohydrate content: 9 g per 100 g

Fiber content: 3.8 g per 100 g

Protein: 3.4 g per 100 g

Fat content: 0.5 g per 100 g

Serving Size: 1 cup cooked (about 150 g)

Glycemic load (GL): Very low

Special Benefits: Rich in fiber, vitamins C, K and A, contains antioxidant compounds such as kaempferol, which may help reduce inflammation. Brussels sprouts also have sulfur-containing compounds that have potential cancer-preventing properties.

Recommended preparation methods: steaming, roasting, boiling or raw in salads.

Buckwheat

Glycemic Index (GI): 54 (medium)

Carbohydrate content: 71 g per 100 g

Fibre content: 10 g per 100 g

Protein: 13 g per 100 g

Fat content: 3.4 g per 100 g

Serving Size: 1 cup cooked (about 168 g)

Glycemic load (GL): Medium

Special Benefits: Buckwheat is an excellent source of fiber and protein, which can help control blood sugar. It also contains important minerals such as magnesium, iron, and zinc, as well as antioxidants that can lower the risk of heart disease and inflammation. Buckwheat is also gluten-free, making it a suitable option for people with celiac disease or gluten intolerance.

Recommended ways of preparation: Boil and use as a side dish, in soups or stews, as a base for porridge or in the form of buckwheat flour for baked goods.

Bulgur

Glycemic Index (GI): 46 (medium)

Carbohydrate content: 17 g per 100 g

Fibre content: 4.5 g per 100 g

Protein: 3.1 g per 100 g

Fat content: 0.2 g per 100 g

Serving Size: 1 cup cooked (about 140 g)

Glycemic load (GL): Medium

Special benefits: Bulgur is a whole grain product that is rich in fiber in addition to a relatively low to medium glycemic index. This combination makes it a long-lasting source of energy and promotes satiety, which is especially important for type 2 diabetics. Fiber also helps to stabilize blood sugar levels and support digestion. In addition, bulgur provides essential vitamins and minerals such as B vitamins, iron and magnesium, which are important for overall health and well-being.

Recommended ways to prepare it: Bulgur is versatile and can be prepared in several ways:

- **Cooking**: Cook bulgur in boiling water or broth. The ratio is usually 1 part bulgur to 2 parts liquid.

- **Soaking**: For salads like tabbouleh, bulgur can simply be soaked in hot water until it is soft.

- **Soups and stews**: Bulgur can also be used as a filling ingredient in soups and stews to increase nutritional value.

- **Stir-fry or oven dishes**: In hearty stir-fries or casseroles, bulgur can serve as an alternative to rice or pasta.

Its versatility and health benefits make bulgur an excellent choice for people with type 2 diabetes who are looking for a balanced yet carbohydrate-controlled diet.

Carrots

Glycemic Index (GI): 35-49 (low to medium)

Carbohydrate content: 10 g per 100 g

Fiber content: 2.8 g per 100 g

Protein: 0.9 g per 100 g

Fat content: 0.2 g per 100 g

Serving Size: 1 cup chopped (about 130 g)

Glycemic Load (GL): Low

Special advantages:

Carrots are rich in beta-carotene, which is converted to vitamin A in the body and helps maintain eye health. They also contain a variety of antioxidants, including polyphenols, which have anti-inflammatory properties. In addition, carrots are a good source of fiber, which can aid digestion and help regulate blood sugar levels. Their low to medium glycemic index makes them suitable for a diabetic diet.

Recommended ways to prepare: Carrots can be enjoyed in a variety of ways. They can be eaten raw as a snack or in salads. Steaming or boiling is also a popular way to serve them as a side dish. Baked or roasted, carrots become a delicious and nutritious side dish. They can also be used in soups, stews and many other dishes.

Cashew nuts

Glycemic Index (GI): 22 (low)

Carbohydrate content: 30 g per 100 g

Fibre content: 3.3 g per 100 g

Protein: 18 g per 100 g

Fat content: 44 g per 100 g

Serving Size: 28 g (about a handful)

Glycemic Load (GL): Low

Special benefits: Cashews are an excellent source of monounsaturated fatty acids, which can support the cardiovascular system. They also contain important minerals such as magnesium, phosphorus, and iron, as well as antioxidant compounds such as vitamin E and phenols, which can help stabilize blood sugar levels and reduce inflammation.

Recommended preparation methods: Raw as a snack, roasted without added salt or sugar, in salads, as an ingredient in stir-fries or as a base for cashew butter and cashew milk.

Notes: Despite the relatively high fat content, cashews are a healthy addition to the diet of diabetics. However, a moderate portion size is important to keep track of calorie intake. The fiber and proteins it contains can also help to promote a long-lasting feeling of satiety.

Cauliflower

Glycemic Index (GI): 15 (low)

Carbohydrate content: 5 g per 100 g

Fibre content: 2 g per 100 g

Protein: 2 g per 100 g

Fat content: 0.3 g per 100 g

Serving Size: 1 cup cooked (about 125 g)

Glycemic load (GL): Very low

Special benefits: Cauliflower is high in fiber and contains numerous vitamins and minerals, including vitamin C, vitamin K, and folate. It also contains antioxidants and compounds such as sulforaphane, which may have anti-inflammatory properties.

Recommended ways to prepare cauliflower: Cauliflower can be prepared in a variety of ways. Popular methods include steaming, boiling, roasting, pureeing, or raw in salads. It can also be used as a healthy alternative to more carbohydrate-rich foods, such as cauliflower rice or cauliflower puree.

Cayenne pepper

Glycemic Index (GI): 15 (very low)

Carbohydrate content: 5 g per 100 g

Fiber content: 1.8 g per 100 g

Protein: 2 g per 100 g

Fat content: 0.4 g per 100 g

Serving Size: 1 teaspoon ground (about 2 g)

Glycemic load (GL): Very low

Special benefits: Cayenne pepper contains capsaicin, an active ingredient that can stimulate metabolism and support fat burning. In addition, cayenne pepper has anti-inflammatory properties and can improve blood circulation. The high antioxidant content can help fight free radicals and boost the immune system.

Recommended preparation methods: Can be used fresh, dried or ground. Cayenne pepper is great for seasoning soups, stews, sauces, and marinades. It can also provide a spicy kick in salads or smoothies.

Note: Due to its spiciness, cayenne pepper should be used in moderation, especially for those with sensitive stomachs or existing gastrointestinal complaints.

Celery

Glycemic Index (GI): 15 (low)

Carbohydrate content: 3 g per 100 g

Fibre content: 1.6 g per 100 g

Protein: 0.7 g per 100 g

Fat content: 0.2 g per 100 g

Serving Size: 1 cup (about 101 g)

Glycemic load (GL): Very low

Special benefits: Celery is known for its extremely low calorie content and is often referred to as a "negative calorie food" because the body expends more energy on digestion than is present in the plant itself. It is rich in fiber and contains a significant amount of vitamin K, vitamin A, and folate. Celery also has anti-inflammatory properties and is a good source of antioxidants, including vitamin C and flavonoids. This composition can help regulate blood sugar levels and reduce the risk of cardiovascular disease.

Recommended preparation methods: Celery can be eaten raw, for example as a crunchy snack or in salads. It is also great for steaming, boiling or steaming. In addition, celery can be used in soups, stews or as part of a vegetable mix. Eat it on its own or alongside a low-fat dip like hummus or yogurt to vary the flavor and get extra nutrients.

Chard

Glycemic Index (GI): 15 (low)

Carbohydrate content: 3.7 g per 100 g

Fibre content: 1.6 g per 100 g

Protein: 1.8 g per 100 g

Fat content: 0.2 g per 100 g

Serving Size: 1 cup cooked (about 175 g)

Glycemic load (GL): Very low

Special benefits: Swiss chard is rich in vitamin K, vitamin A and vitamin C and contains various antioxidants and minerals such as magnesium, iron and calcium. These nutrients are important for blood sugar regulation, supporting bone health, and promoting a healthy immune system. Also, chard contains betalains, which are known for their anti-inflammatory properties.

Recommended ways to prepare: Steam, lightly sauté or use in soups and stews.

Swiss chard can also be enjoyed raw in salads, especially if the leaves are young and tender.

Chayote

Glycemic Index (GI): 20 (low)

Carbohydrate content: 4.5 g per 100 g

Fiber content: 1.7 g per 100 g

Protein: 1 g per 100 g

Fat content: 0.2 g per 100 g

Serving Size: 1 cup cooked (about 150 g)

Glycemic load (GL): Very low

Special benefits: Chayote is low in calories and rich in vitamins, especially vitamin C and B vitamins such as folate. It also contains essential minerals such as potassium and magnesium. Additionally, it provides antioxidants that can reduce oxidative stress and promote cellular health. Chayote is also hydrating because it has a high water content.

Recommended preparation methods: steaming, boiling, roasting or raw in salads.

Cherries

Glycemic Index (GI): 22 (low)

Carbohydrate content: 16 g per 100 g

Fibre content: 2 g per 100 g

Protein: 1 g per 100 g

Fat content: 0.3 g per 100 g

Serving Size: 1 cup pitted (about 154 g)

Glycemic Load (GL): Low

Special benefits: Cherries are rich in antioxidants, especially anthocyanins, which have anti-inflammatory properties. They also contain vitamin C, potassium and melatonin, which can help regulate sleep. Cherries may help reduce oxidative stress through their antioxidant effects, and their anti-inflammatory effects may reduce the risk of certain chronic diseases, including cardiovascular disease.

Recommended preparation methods: Fresh and raw as a snack, in fruit salads, smoothies or even as an ingredient in desserts. Cherries can also be cooked and used in sauces or as a side dish.

Chia seeds

Glycemic Index (GI): 1 (very low)

Carbohydrate content: 42 g per 100 g

Fiber content: 34 g per 100 g

Protein: 16 g per 100 g

Fat content: 31 g per 100 g

Serving Size: 1 tablespoon (about 12 g)

Glycemic load (GL): Very low

Special advantages:

- Rich in fiber, which can help regulate blood sugar levels.

- Contains omega-3 fatty acids, which may have a positive effect on heart health.

- Provides a good source of plant-based protein, which is important for muscle building and repair.

- Contains antioxidants that can prevent cell damage caused by free radicals.

- Rich in minerals such as calcium, magnesium and phosphorus, which contribute to bone health.

Recommended preparation methods:

- Can be sprinkled raw over yogurt, porridge or salads.

- Great for making chia pudding by soaking it in liquid (such as milk, almond milk, or water).

- Can be used as an egg substitute in baking recipes when soaked in water (1 tablespoon chia seeds with 3 tablespoons water).

- Can be blended into smoothies to provide extra nutrients.

Chicken

Glycemic Index (GI): 0 (no effect on blood sugar levels)

Carbohydrate content: 0 g per 100 g

Fiber content: 0 g per 100 g

Protein: 31 g per 100 g

Fat content: 3.6 g per 100 g

Serving Size: 1 small chicken breast, cooked (approx. 100-150 g)

Glycemic load (GL): Very low

Special benefits: Chicken breast is an excellent source of lean protein, which is important for building muscle and maintaining muscle mass. It is low in saturated fats and contains no carbohydrates, which makes it particularly beneficial for people with type 2 diabetes who need to control their blood sugar levels. It also provides important nutrients such as B vitamins (especially niacin and vitamin B6).

Recommended preparation methods: grilling, baking, steaming or boiling. Use minimal oil and prefer healthy preparation methods to avoid extra fat content. You can also use the chicken breast in salads, soups, or stews. Be careful not to bread them or marinate them in high-sugar marinades to maximize the health benefits.

Chickpeas

Glycemic Index (GI): 28-32 (low)

Carbohydrate content: 27 g per 100 g (cooked)

Fiber content: 7.6 g per 100 g (cooked)

Protein: 8.9 g per 100 g (cooked)

Fat content: 2.6 g per 100 g (cooked)

Serving Size: 1 cup cooked (about 164 g)

Glycemic Load (GL): Low

Special benefits: Chickpeas are rich in fiber and vegetable protein, which contributes to a lasting feeling of satiety and can stabilize blood sugar levels. They also contain valuable micronutrients such as folic acid, iron, magnesium and zinc. The fiber in chickpeas promotes healthy digestion and may help reduce the risk of heart disease.

Recommended preparation methods: Chickpeas can be used in many ways, for example in salads, stews, soups or as a base for hummus. They can also be eaten roasted as a healthy snack. If they are used from the can, they should be rinsed well to reduce the sodium content.

Chicory

Glycemic Index (GI): 15 (low)

Carbohydrate content: 4 g per 100 g

Fibre content: 3 g per 100 g

Protein: 1.7 g per 100 g

Fat content: 0.2 g per 100 g

Serving Size: 1 cup raw (about 50 g)

Glycemic load (GL): Very low

Special Benefits: Chicory is high in fiber and contains a variety of vitamins and minerals, including vitamin A, vitamin C, vitamin K, and folate. It is also an excellent source of inulin, a special type of soluble fiber that can support the growth of healthy gut bacteria. Chicory can help regulate blood sugar levels, which is especially beneficial for people with type 2 diabetes.

Recommended ways of preparation: Raw chicory can be used excellently in salads. Its slightly bitter taste can be offset by combining it with sweeter ingredients such as fruit or a sweet vinaigrette. Chicory can also be steamed, grilled, or lightly seared and used as a side dish or in main courses.

In addition to being a nutrient-dense and versatile ingredient, chicory helps promote healthy digestion and stable blood sugar levels.

Chili

Glycemic Index (GI): 6 (very low)

Carbohydrate content: 9 g per 100 g

Fiber content: 1.5 g per 100 g

Protein: 0.9 g per 100 g

Fat content: 0.2 g per 100 g

Serving Size: 1 cup raw (about 120 g)

Glycemic load (GL): Very low

Special advantages:

Chili contains capsaicin, a substance known to boost metabolism and help burn fat. Capsaicin can also help regulate appetite and thus help manage body weight, which can be especially beneficial for type 2 diabetics. In addition, chili is rich in vitamin C and antioxidants, which can help support the immune system and reduce inflammation.

Recommended preparation methods:

Chili can be used fresh, dried, or as a powder to add flavor and spiciness to various dishes. It is well suited for seasoning soups, stews, sauces and marinades. Fresh chillies can also be used in salads or as a topping for various dishes.

Note: Since chili can be very hot, consumption should be adjusted individually, especially for people with sensitive stomachs or gastrointestinal complaints.

Chinese cabbage

Glycemic Index (GI): 32 (low)

Carbohydrate content: 4 g per 100 g

Fiber content: 1.5 g per 100 g

Protein: 1.2 g per 100 g

Fat content: 0.2 g per 100 g

Serving Size: 1 cup raw (about 75 g)

Glycemic load (GL): Very low

Special benefits: Chinese cabbage is an excellent source of vitamins C and K, contains many antioxidants and bioactive compounds known for their anti-inflammatory properties. It also has a high water content that helps hydrate and is low in calories, making it an ideal choice for a calorie-controlled diet.

Recommended preparation methods: Raw in salads, steamed, lightly fried or as an ingredient in soups and stews.

Chives

Glycemic Index (GI): 1 (very low)

Carbohydrate content: 4.4 g per 100 g

Fiber content: 2.5 g per 100 g

Protein: 3.3 g per 100 g

Fat content: 0.7 g per 100 g

Serving Size: 1 tablespoon freshly chopped (about 10 g)

Glycemic load (GL): Very low

Special benefits: Chives are low in calories and rich in vitamins A, C and K. It also contains antioxidants and compounds such as allicin, which may have antihypertensive and cholesterol-lowering properties.

Recommended preparation methods: Freshly chopped as a garnish for soups, salads, potato dishes or egg dishes. It can also be used in sauces, dips or herb butters.

Note: Chives not only bring flavor and color to the dish, but also health benefits. The fiber it contains supports digestion, while the vitamins can strengthen the immune system. It is an excellent addition to a balanced diet for type 2 diabetes.

Chokeberries

Glycemic Index (GI): 25 (low)

Carbohydrate content: 15 g per 100 g

Fibre content: 5.3 g per 100 g

Protein: 1.4 g per 100 g

Fat content: 0.4 g per 100 g

Serving Size: 1/2 cup (about 75 g)

Glycemic load (GL): Very low

Special benefits: Chokeberries are an excellent source of antioxidants, especially polyphenols and anthocyanins, which can reduce oxidative stress. They also contain high amounts of vitamin C and manganese, which help boost the immune system and bone health. In addition, they may have anti-inflammatory properties and support heart health.

Recommended preparation methods: Chokeberries can be eaten fresh or dried. They are ideal for smoothies, salads, yoghurt, muesli bars or as an addition to baked goods. They are also popular as juice or jam.

Chokeberries offer a variety of health benefits that may be especially beneficial for type 2 diabetics. Their low glycemic load helps keep blood sugar levels stable.

Cinnamon

Glycemic Index (GI): 5 (very low)

Carbohydrate content: 81 g per 100 g

Fibre content: 53 g per 100 g

Protein: 4 g per 100 g

Fat content: 1.2 g per 100 g

Serving Size: 1 teaspoon ground (about 2.6 g)

Glycemic load (GL): Very low

Special benefits: Cinnamon is low in calories, high in fiber and contains numerous antioxidants. Studies suggest that cinnamon may improve insulin sensitivity and stabilize blood sugar levels in type 2 diabetics. In addition, it is said to have an anti-inflammatory effect.

Recommended Preparation Methods: Cinnamon can be used as a spice in various dishes, including oatmeal, smoothies, teas, curries and baked goods. Adding it to fresh fruit or yogurt is also a popular method of use.

Clementines

Glycemic Index (GI): 30 (low)

Carbohydrate content: 12 g per 100 g

Fiber content: 1.7 g per 100 g

Protein: 0.8 g per 100 g

Fat content: 0.2 g per 100 g

Serving Size: 1 clementine (approx. 74 g)

Glycemic Load (GL): Low

Special benefits: Rich in vitamin C, which strengthens the immune system and has antioxidant properties. They also contain potassium, which can help regulate blood pressure, and are also juicy and naturally sweet, making them an ideal, healthy snack for diabetics.

Recommended preparation methods: Fresh and pure, in fruit salads or as part of savory dishes. They can also be used as a natural sweetener in desserts and smoothies.

Cocoa (unsweetened)

Glycemic Index (GI): 20-25 (low)

Carbohydrate content: 58 g per 100 g

Fibre content: 33 g per 100 g

Protein: 19.6 g per 100 g

Fat content: 11 g per 100 g

Serving Size: 1 tbsp (approx. 10 g)

Glycemic load (GL): Very low

Special advantages:

- **Rich in fiber:** Aids digestion and can help stabilize blood sugar levels.

- **Contains flavonoids:** These antioxidants can reduce inflammation and contribute to heart health.

- **Source of magnesium:** Supports muscle function and energy metabolism.

- **Mood-boosting effect:** Theobromine and phenylethylamine can improve mood.

-

Recommended preparation methods:

- **In smoothies:** To increase nutritional value and add a chocolaty note.

- **In baked goods:** For a healthier alternative to sweetened cocoa in muffins, brownies or cookies.

- **As a hot drink:** Unsweetened cocoa with an alternative such as stevia or another sweetener.

- **In yoghurts or oatmeal:** For a chocolatey taste with additional nutrients.

Cacao (unsweetened) is an excellent ingredient for type 2 diabetics who are looking for a healthy, tasty, and nutrient-dense addition to their diet.

Cocoa beans (raw)

Glycemic Index (GI): 20 (low)

Carbohydrate content: 57 g per 100 g

Fibre content: 33 g per 100 g

Protein: 13 g per 100 g

Fat content: 49 g per 100 g

Serving Size: 1 tablespoon (about 15 g)

Glycemic Load (GL): Low to moderate

Special Benefits: Cocoa beans are rich in fiber and antioxidants, especially flavonoids, which can help improve insulin sensitivity. They also contain magnesium, iron, and other minerals that are important for overall health. Raw cacao can help lower blood pressure and promote cardiovascular health, which can be especially beneficial for diabetics.

Recommended preparation methods: Cocoa beans can be eaten raw, for example as a snack or mixed into smoothies and shakes. They are also popular as ingredients in baked goods or desserts. To maximize the health benefits, one should prefer raw or minimally processed forms.

Cocoa powder (unsweetened)

Glycemic Index (GI): 20 (low)

Carbohydrate content: 57 g per 100 g

Fibre content: 33 g per 100 g

Protein: 20 g per 100 g

Fat content: 11 g per 100 g

Serving Size: 1 tablespoon (about 5 g)

Glycemic load (GL): Very low

Special benefits: Cocoa powder is rich in fiber, magnesium, iron and antioxidants, especially flavonoids. These promote heart health, improve insulin sensitivity and reduce the risk of inflammation.

Recommended Preparation Methods: Can be added to smoothies, yogurt, oatmeal, or baked goods to enhance flavor and nutritional content. Ideal in combination with foods that do not contain added sugars.

Coconut

Glycemic Index (GI): Very low

Carbohydrate content: 15 g per 100 g

Fiber content: 9 g per 100 g

Protein: 3.3 g per 100 g

Fat content: 33 g per 100 g

Serving Size: 1 cup grated/shredded (about 80 g)

Glycemic Load (GL): Low

Special advantages:

- Rich in fiber that promotes digestion

- Contains medium-chain fatty acids (MCFA), which are easy to digest and can serve as a quick source of energy

- Provides a good source of minerals such as manganese, iron, and copper

- Coenzyme Q10 and other antioxidants support cell health and can reduce inflammation

- Contains lauric acid, which has antimicrobial properties

Recommended preparation methods:

- Stir into smoothies or mueslis

- Use as coconut flour for baking

- Use coconut oil for cooking, baking or as an ingredient in dressings

- Fresh coconut water as a hydrating drink

- Add coconut milk to curries or soups

Coconut flour

Glycemic Index (GI): 51 (medium)

Carbohydrate content: 18 g per 100 g

Fibre content: 38 g per 100 g

Protein: 19 g per 100 g

Fat content: 14 g per 100 g

Serving Size: 1/4 cup (about 30 g)

Glycemic Load (GL): Low

Special benefits: Coconut flour is rich in fiber, which promotes digestion and ensures longer-lasting satiety. It also contains healthy fats that can positively affect cholesterol levels, as well as proteins that help build muscle. Furthermore, coconut flour brings a pleasant coconut flavor to your dishes and has fewer carbohydrates compared to traditional wheat flour, making it an excellent option for type 2 diabetics.

Recommended preparation methods: Coconut flour can be used in many ways. It is great for baking bread, cakes and muffins, but also for thickening sauces and soups. However, it absorbs more liquid than traditional flour, so you should adjust the amount of liquid in your recipes accordingly.

Coconut milk (unsweetened)

Glycemic Index (GI): 40 (low)

Carbohydrate content: 2.7 g per 100 ml

Fibre content: trace

Protein: 2.3 g per 100 ml

Fat content: 17.3 g per 100 ml

Serving Size: 1 cup (about 240 ml)

Glycemic Load (GL): Low

Special benefits: Unsweetened coconut milk is rich in medium-chain triglycerides (MCTs), which are easy to digest and can be quickly converted into energy. It also contains iron, magnesium and potassium, which contribute to overall health. Coconut milk also offers a creamy consistency and natural flavor that can enhance many dishes.

Recommended preparation methods: Can be used in smoothies, soups, curry dishes, desserts or as a milk alternative in coffee and tea.

Coconut oil

Glycemic Index (GI): 0 (not relevant)

Carbohydrate content: 0 g per 100 g

Fiber content: 0 g per 100 g

Protein: 0 g per 100 g

Fat content: 100 g per 100 g

Serving Size: 1 tablespoon (about 14 g)

Glycemic load (GL): Not relevant (as no carbohydrates)

Special benefits: Coconut oil consists mainly of medium-chain triglycerides (MCTs), which can be quickly used by the body for energy instead of being stored as fat. It has anti-inflammatory properties and can increase HDL (good) cholesterol. It also contains lauric acid, which has antimicrobial and antiviral properties.

Recommended ways to prepare: Frying: Coconut oil has a high smoke point, making it good for frying and deep-frying.

- **Baking:** It can be used as a substitute for butter or other oils in baking recipes.

- **Raw:** Can be added to smoothies, coffee, or as a spread on bread.

However, coconut oil should be used in moderation because it contains a high percentage of saturated fat. Diabetics should consume it as part of a balanced diet and pay attention to a total fat intake to prevent cardiovascular disease.

Coconut water (unsweetened)

Glycemic Index (GI): 3 (very low)

Carbohydrate content: 3.7 g per 100 ml

Fibre content: 0 g per 100 ml

Protein: 0.7 g per 100 ml

Fat content: 0.2 g per 100 ml

Serving Size: 1 cup (about 240 ml)

Glycemic load (GL): Very low

Special benefits: Coconut water is low in calories and an excellent source of electrolytes such as potassium and magnesium. It helps balance electrolyte balance in the body and can improve hydration. It also contains small amounts of vitamins and minerals that can contribute to overall health. Due to its low carbohydrate and calorie content, it is an excellent option for diabetics to meet fluid needs without significantly affecting blood sugar levels. In addition, it can help support the cardiovascular system and have a positive impact on blood pressure.

Recommended ways of preparation: Can be consumed directly as a refreshing drink, ideally chilled. It can also be used as a base for smoothies or as a substitute for water in various recipes to add extra flavor.

Please note that sweetened coconut water can contain significantly higher amounts of sugar and carbohydrates, making it less suitable for diabetics. Therefore, always make sure to choose unsweetened coconut water.

Coriander

Glycemic Index (GI): 5 (very low)

Carbohydrate content: 3.7 g per 100 g

Fiber content: 2.8 g per 100 g

Protein: 2.1 g per 100 g

Fat content: 0.6 g per 100 g

Serving Size: 1/4 cup freshly chopped (about 4 g)

Glycemic load (GL): Very low

Special benefits: Coriander is rich in antioxidants and vitamin K. It contains beneficial bioactive compounds that can have anti-inflammatory and antimicrobial effects. It can also help to positively influence blood sugar levels, which is especially beneficial for diabetics. Coriander is also often prized for its digestive properties.

Recommended ways to prepare: Cilantro can be used fresh as a garnish for a variety of dishes, including salads, soups, and salsas. It can also be used in smoothies, marinades or as an ingredient in spice mixes and sauces. Another popular application is to add it to various dips such as guacamole or hummus.

Corncob

Glycemic Index (GI): 52 (moderate)

Carbohydrate content: 19 g per 100 g

Fibre content: 2.7 g per 100 g

Protein: 3.4 g per 100 g

Fat content: 1.5 g per 100 g

Serving Size: 1 corn on the cob (approx. 100 g)

Glycemic load (GL): Medium

Special benefits: Corn on the cob is a good source of fiber, which can help maintain healthy digestion. They also contain a wide range of vitamins and minerals, including B vitamins, magnesium, and antioxidants such as lutein and zeaxanthin. These antioxidants support eye health and can reduce the risk of chronic diseases.

Recommended preparation methods: Grilled, steamed or boiled. Avoid preparing corn with too much butter or high-fat toppings to keep the fat content low.

Cottage cheese (low fat)

Glycemic Index (GI): 10 (very low)

Carbohydrate content: 3.4 g per 100 g

Fiber content: 0 g per 100 g

Protein: 11.1 g per 100 g

Fat content: 1.2 g per 100 g

Serving Size: 1/2 cup (about 100 g)

Glycemic load (GL): Very low

Special advantages:

- Rich in protein, it supports muscle building and recovery.

- Low fat content, ideal for a calorie-conscious diet.

- Good source of calcium, important for strong bones and teeth.

Recommended preparation methods:

- Ready to eat, ideal as a snack.

- Can be combined with vegetables or fruits.

- Can be used in salads or as a filling in wholemeal wraps.

Courgette

Glycemic Index (GI): 15 (low)

Carbohydrate content: 3.1 g per 100 g

Fibre content: 1 g per 100 g

Protein: 1.2 g per 100 g

Fat content: 0.2 g per 100 g

Serving Size: 1 cup cooked (about 180 g)

Glycemic load (GL): Very low

Special benefits: Zucchini is low in calories, rich in vitamins, especially vitamin C and vitamin A, as well as minerals such as potassium and manganese. It also contains antioxidants and is easy to digest.

Recommended preparation methods: Steaming, grilling, roasting or raw spiralized in salads as a low-carb substitute for pasta.

Zucchini is an excellent food for type 2 diabetics, as it has a low glycemic index and a very low glycemic load. The low carbohydrate and calorie levels help maintain stable blood sugar levels and control weight, which is crucial for blood sugar control. The fiber it contains contributes to satiety and promotes healthy digestion. The versatility of the preparation options makes zucchini an ideal part of a healthy diet.

Cranberries (unsweetened)

Glycemic Index (GI): 45 (low)

Carbohydrate content: 12 g per 100 g

Fiber content: 5 g per 100 g

Protein: 0.4 g per 100 g

Fat content: 0.1 g per 100 g

Serving Size: 1 cup (about 100 g)

Glycemic Load (GL): Low

Special Benefits: Rich in vitamins C and E, contains many antioxidants and anthocyanins that can help reduce inflammation and promote heart health. Supports urinary tract health.

Recommended preparation methods: Fresh in salads, smoothies, as a snack or in combination with other fruits and nuts.

Note: When buying cranberries, make sure that they are unsweetened to avoid adding unnecessary sugar.

Cucumbers

Glycemic Index (GI): 15 (low)

Carbohydrate content: 4 g per 100 g

Fibre content: 0.5 g per 100 g

Protein: 0.6 g per 100 g

Fat content: 0.1 g per 100 g

Serving Size: 1 cup sliced (about 120 g)

Glycemic load (GL): Very low

Special advantages:

- Very low in calories and therefore well suited for weight control, which is important for type 2 diabetes.

- High water content (about 95%), which contributes to hydration.

- Good supplier of vitamin K, which is important for blood clotting and bone health.

- Contains antioxidants such as beta-carotene and flavonoids that can reduce inflammation.

Recommended preparation methods:

- Raw in salads or as a snack.

- Pickled as cucumber pickles (pay attention to the sugar content in the brine).

- In smoothies for extra hydration and nutrition.

- As an addition to sandwiches and wraps for extra crunch.

Cucumbers are an excellent choice for people with type 2 diabetes because they do not greatly affect blood sugar levels and can be used in a variety of ways in the diet.

Currants (black, red, white)

Glycemic Index (GI): 22-24 (low)

Carbohydrate content: 6-10 g per 100 g (depending on the variety)

Fiber content: 4-5 g per 100 g

Protein: 1-1.5 g per 100 g

Fat content: 0.3-0.5 g per 100 g

Serving Size: 1 cup (about 112 g)

Glycemic load (GL): Very low

Special advantages:

- Rich in fiber, which aids digestion and promotes a longer feeling of satiety.

- High vitamin C content, especially in blackcurrants, supports the immune system.

- Contain a variety of antioxidants, including anthocyanins in blackcurrants, which have anti-inflammatory properties and can promote blood vessel health.

- Source of vitamin K and manganese, which are important for healthy bones and blood clotting.

Recommended preparation methods:

- Fresh as a snack or in a fruit salad.

- Canned as jam with little or no added sugar.

- In smoothies to add a nutrient-rich and refreshing character.

- As a topping for yoghurt, oatmeal or muesli.

- For refining hearty dishes such as sauerkraut or meat sauces to achieve a sour-fruity note.

Curry powder

Properties:

Glycemic Index (GI): Curry powder is made up of a mixture of spices and has no direct effect on blood sugar levels. Therefore, it does not have a glycemic index.

Carbohydrate content: Almost negligible, as they are primarily spices.

Fiber content: Low, varies by blend, but typically less than 1g per teaspoon.

Protein: Very low, usually less than 1 g per teaspoon.

Fat content: Low, varies by blend, but typically less than 1g per teaspoon.

Serving Size: Typical is 1 teaspoon (about 2-3 g).

Special advantages:

- Contains a variety of antioxidants and anti-inflammatory compounds that come from the individual spices, such as curcumin from turmeric.

- Can improve the taste of food without adding significant calories or carbohydrates, which is especially beneficial for diabetics.

- Various studies suggest that some of the spices in curry powder, such as turmeric and fennel, may help improve insulin sensitivity.

Recommended preparation methods:

- Curry powder can be used in a variety of ways in the kitchen. It is ideal for curries, stews, soups or as a condiment for meat, fish and vegetables.

- Can also be used in marinades, dressings or to flavor rice and legumes.

Dandelion leaves

Glycemic Index (GI): 15 (low)

Carbohydrate content: 9 g per 100 g

Fibre content: 3.5 g per 100 g

Protein: 2.7 g per 100 g

Fat content: 0.6 g per 100 g

Serving Size: 1 cup raw (about 55 g)

Glycemic load (GL): Very low

Special benefits: Dandelion leaves are rich in fiber, which can help regulate blood sugar levels. They contain a variety of vitamins and minerals, including vitamins A, C, and K, as well as iron and calcium. In addition, they are a good source of antioxidants, which can help reduce inflammation and promote overall health.

Recommended preparation methods: Raw in salads, as an ingredient in green smoothies, lightly steamed or as a tea.

Dark chocolate (min. 70% cocoa)

Glycemic Index (GI): 25 (low)

Carbohydrate content: 46 g per 100 g

Fibre content: 11 g per 100 g

Protein: 8 g per 100 g

Fat content: 43 g per 100 g

Serving Size: 30 g (about 3-4 pieces)

Glycemic Load (GL): Medium to low (depending on serving size)

Special advantages:

- Rich in antioxidants, especially flavonoids, which can lower the risk of heart disease.

- Contains magnesium, which is important for blood sugar metabolism and heart health.

- May help stabilize insulin levels and reduce food cravings.

Recommended preparation methods:

- Pure as a small snack.

- In small quantities as an ingredient in desserts to reduce the total amount of sugar.

- Grated or melted over fruits or nuts.

Dark chocolate with a cocoa content of at least 70% can be a healthy treat if consumed in moderation. It offers a tasty way to enrich the diet while benefiting from its health benefits.

Dates

Glycemic Index (GI): 42-55 (medium, varies by variety)

Carbohydrate content: 75 g per 100 g

Fiber content: 6.7 g per 100 g

Protein: 2 g per 100 g

Fat content: 0.2 g per 100 g

Serving Size: 1-2 dates (approx. 20-30 g)

Glycemic load (GL): Medium

Special benefits: Dates are a good source of fiber, potassium, magnesium, and antioxidants such as flavonoids, carotenoids, and phenolic acids. They offer a natural sweetness and can be used as a healthier alternative to refined sugar.

Recommended preparation methods: In moderation as a snack, in smoothies, as a natural sweetener in baked goods or as an ingredient in savory dishes such as chutneys and stews.

Dill

Glycemic Index (GI): 5 (very low)

Carbohydrate content: 2 g per 100 g

Fiber content: 2.1 g per 100 g

Protein: 3.5 g per 100 g

Fat content: 1.1 g per 100 g

Serving Size: 1 tablespoon fresh (about 1 g)

Glycemic load (GL): Very low

Special advantages:

- Rich in vitamins A and C that help strengthen the immune system.

- Contains valuable antioxidants that can help reduce oxidative stress.

- Promotes digestion and can relieve flatulence and stomach cramps.

- Dill has anti-inflammatory properties that can help reduce inflammation in the body.

Recommended preparation methods:

- Use as a fresh herb in salads, soups or sauces.

- Particularly suitable for seasoning fish dishes.

- Can also be used dried, but retains the best flavor and nutrients when fresh.

Note for diabetics type 2:

Dill is an excellent spice for type 2 diabetics because it contains hardly any carbohydrates and does not affect blood sugar levels. Its antioxidant and anti-inflammatory properties may additionally provide health benefits.

Dried fruit (in moderation and without added sugar)

Glycemic Index (GI): Varies depending on the fruit, usually medium to high

Carbohydrate content: 60-75 g per 100 g

Fiber content: 7-15 g per 100 g

Protein: 1-5 g per 100 g

Fat content: 0-3 g per 100 g

Serving Size: A small handful or about 30 g

Glycemic load (GL): Varies depending on the fruit, usually medium-high

Special advantages:

- Dried fruits are rich in fiber, which aids digestion.

- They contain a variety of vitamins and minerals, including potassium, magnesium, and iron.

- With no added sugar, dried fruit can be a nutrient-dense snack option.

- Contain antioxidants that can help reduce oxidative stress.

Recommended preparation methods:

- Consume in moderation as a snack.

- Add in small quantities to cereals, salads or yoghurt.

- To refine baked goods, however, make sure that the total amount of sugar in the recipe remains within limits.

Edamame

Glycemic Index (GI): 18 (low)

Carbohydrate content: 8 g per 100 g

Fiber content: 5 g per 100 g

Protein: 11 g per 100 g

Fat content: 5 g per 100 g

Serving Size: 1 cup cooked (about 155 g)

Glycemic load (GL): Very low

Special benefits: Edamame is rich in vegetable protein, fiber, and various vitamins and minerals, including iron, magnesium, potassium, and vitamin K. They also contain isoflavones, plant compounds that may have antioxidant and anti-inflammatory properties.

Recommended preparation methods: Steamed or cooked as a snack, in salads or as an ingredient in various dishes such as soups, stews and stir-fries.

Edamame are an excellent choice for people with type 2 diabetes due to their low glycemic index and high fiber and protein content. They can help stabilize blood sugar levels and promote a long-lasting feeling of satiety.

Egg whites (clear)

Glycemic Index (GI): 0 (none)

Carbohydrate content: 0.2 g per 100 g

Fiber content: 0 g per 100 g

Protein: 10.9 g per 100 g

Fat content: 0.2 g per 100 g

Serving Size: 1 egg white (approx. 33 g)

Glycemic load (GL): Very low

Special advantages:

- Rich in high-quality protein, which is important for building muscle and repairing tissues.

- Very low in calories and fat, ideal for a calorie-conscious diet.

- No carbohydrates, which means that it does not cause blood sugar fluctuations.

Recommended preparation methods:

- Can be consumed raw or used in various cooking methods such as boiling, poaching, or baking.

- Also ideal for the preparation of egg white omelets, in salads or as an ingredient in baked goods to increase their protein content.

Additional note:

Since protein (clearly) contains very little fat and no carbohydrates, it is particularly suitable as a protein source for people with type 2 diabetes. It provides a way to increase protein intake without additional calorie or carbohydrate intake.

Egg yolks (in moderation)

Glycemic Index (GI): 0 (low)

Carbohydrate content: Almost 0 g per 100 g

Fiber content: 0 g per 100 g

Protein: 15 g per 100 g

Fat content: 27 g per 100 g

Serving Size: 1 egg yolk (approx. 17 g)

Glycemic load (GL): Very low

Special benefits: Egg yolks are rich in essential nutrients such as vitamin A, vitamin D, vitamin E, vitamin K and choline. It also contains important healthy fats, including omega-3 fatty acids, as well as antioxidants such as lutein and zeaxanthin, which may support eye health.

Recommended Preparation Methods: Egg yolks can be used in numerous dishes, including scrambled eggs, boiled eggs, egg salads, or as an ingredient in dressings and sauces. Since egg yolks have a high cholesterol content, it is recommended to consume them in moderation, especially for those with type 2 diabetes or other cardiovascular risks.

Egg yolks are a nutritious addition to a balanced diet, but they should be used moderately in the context of the overall fat and cholesterol content of the diet.

Eggplant

Glycemic Index (GI): 15 (low)

Carbohydrate content: 6 g per 100 g

Fibre content: 3 g per 100 g

Protein: 1 g per 100 g

Fat content: 0.2 g per 100 g

Serving Size: 1 cup cooked (about 100 g)

Glycemic load (GL): Very low

Special benefits: Eggplants are rich in fiber and antioxidants such as nasunin, an anthocyanin found in the peel that can protect cell membranes from damage. They are also a source of vitamins such as vitamins B6 and K, as well as minerals such as manganese. Eggplant can help control blood sugar levels and has anti-inflammatory properties.

Recommended preparation methods: grilling, baking, steaming or as part of stews and casseroles. Use as little oil as possible when cooking, as eggplants tend to absorb a lot of fat.

Eggs

Glycemic Index (GI): 0 (very low)

Carbohydrate content: 0.6 g per 100 g

Fiber content: 0 g per 100 g (eggs do not contain fiber)

Protein: 13 g per 100 g

Fat content: 11 g per 100 g

Serving Size: 1 large egg (approx. 50 g)

Glycemic load (GL): Very low

Special benefits: Eggs are an excellent source of high-quality protein and contain all the essential amino acids that the body needs. They are rich in various vitamins, including vitamins A, D, E, and B12. Eggs also contain minerals such as iron, phosphorus and zinc. The antioxidants found in eggs, such as lutein and zeaxanthin, can promote eye health. Eating eggs can contribute to satiety and thus help with weight management.

Recommended preparation methods: Hard or soft boiled, poached, stirred or as an omelette. To reduce the fat content, frying in large quantities of oil or butter can be dispensed with.

Endive

Glycemic Index (GI): 15 (low)

Carbohydrate content: 3 g per 100 g

Fibre content: 3.1 g per 100 g

Protein: 1.3 g per 100 g

Fat content: 0.2 g per 100 g

Serving Size: 1 cup raw (about 50 g)

Glycemic load (GL): Very low

Special benefits: Endives are low in calories and high in fiber, making them a good choice for blood sugar control. They also contain important vitamins such as vitamin A, vitamin C and vitamin K, as well as minerals such as potassium and folate.

Recommended preparation methods: Raw in salad, steamed or lightly sautéed as a side dish. Endives can also be used as a filling for wraps or in combination with other vegetables to add extra texture and nutrients to dishes.

Fennel

Glycemic Index (GI): 16 (low)

Carbohydrate content: 7.3 g per 100 g

Fibre content: 3.1 g per 100 g

Protein: 1.2 g per 100 g

Fat content: 0.2 g per 100 g

Serving Size: 1 cup raw, sliced (about 87 g)

Glycemic load (GL): Very low

Special benefits: Rich in fiber, vitamin C and potassium, contains anti-inflammatory plant compounds, promotes digestion and can reduce bloating.

Recommended preparation methods: Raw in salads, steamed, roasted in the oven or as an ingredient in soups.

Fennel is particularly popular because of its mildly anise-like taste and can be used in a variety of ways in the kitchen. Thanks to its low glycemic index and low carbohydrate content, it is ideal for the diet of type 2 diabetics. Fennel not only supports the regulation of blood sugar, but also contributes to healthy digestion due to its high fiber content. Additionally, these vegetables provide important nutrients such as vitamin C, which acts as an antioxidant and boosts the immune system, and potassium, which is important for good heart health.

Preparation tips: Roast fennel in the oven with a little olive oil and spices to intensify its natural flavor, or add it raw to a fresh salad for a crunchy texture. Steamed, fennel can also be a perfect side dish or give soups and stews a special touch.

Fish (salmon, tuna, mackerel, herring)

Glycemic Index (GI): 0 (low)

Carbohydrate content: 0 g per 100 g

Fiber content: 0 g per 100 g

Protein: 20-25 g per 100 g

Fat content: 5-15 g per 100 g (depending on the type of fish)

Serving Size: 100 g

Glycemic load (GL): Very low

Special advantages:

- Very rich in high-quality proteins that support muscle growth and maintenance.

- High content of omega-3 fatty acids, which have an anti-inflammatory effect and protect the cardiovascular system.

- Contains important vitamins and minerals such as vitamin D, vitamin B12, selenium and iodine.

- May help lower blood sugar levels and improve insulin sensitivity.

- Supports heart and brain health through omega-3 fatty acids.

Recommended preparation methods:

- Grilled: Quick and easy, preserves the nutrients and gives the fish a delicious texture.

- Baked: Healthy and easy to season to enjoy different flavors.

- Steamed: Gentle preparation method that preserves the natural taste and nutrients of the fish.

- Sashimi (raw): Particularly suitable for fresh salmon or tuna, rich in vitamins and minerals.

- Cooked: A gentle method of preparation that is well suited for fish soups or stews.

Fish is therefore an excellent choice for type 2 diabetics, thanks to its low glycemic index, high-quality proteins and important nutrients that offer a variety of health benefits.

Flax flour

Glycemic Index (GI): Unknown (generally very low as it is mainly made up of fiber)

Carbohydrate content: 29 g per 100 g

Fibre content: 27 g per 100 g

Protein: 18 g per 100 g

Fat content: 42 g per 100 g (many of which are essential omega-3 fatty acids)

Serving Size: 1 tablespoon (about 7 g)

Glycemic load (GL): Very low

Special advantages:

- Rich in fiber, which aids in blood sugar control.

- High content of omega-3 fatty acids, which have anti-inflammatory properties.

- Contains lignans, which have antioxidant effects and can help balance hormones.

- Good source of vegetable protein.

Recommended preparation methods:

- Add to smoothies for a creamy consistency and extra nutritional value.

- Stir into yogurt or oatmeal.

- Use as an egg substitute in baking recipes (1 tablespoon flax flour + 3 tablespoons water = 1 egg).

- Mixing into doughs and doughs for bread, biscuits or other baked goods to improve their nutritional profile.

Frisée

Glycemic Index (GI): 15 (low)

Carbohydrate content: 3 g per 100 g

Fibre content: 3 g per 100 g

Protein: 1.5 g per 100 g

Fat content: 0.2 g per 100 g

Serving Size: 1 cup raw (about 50 g)

Glycemic load (GL): Very low

Special benefits: Frisée is particularly rich in fiber, which can promote healthy digestion and help stabilize blood sugar levels. It's also a good source of vitamin A, vitamin C, and folate. Thanks to its high water content, frisée can contribute to hydration, and it contains very few calories, making it an ideal choice for a calorie-conscious diet.

Recommended ways to prepare: Frisée can be used raw in salads and pairs well with a variety of dressings and ingredients. It can also be lightly sautéed or used in soups and stews to provide extra texture and nutritional value.

Garlic

Glycemic Index (GI): 0 (very low)

Carbohydrate content: 33 g per 100 g

Fiber content: 2.1 g per 100 g

Protein: 6.4 g per 100 g

Fat content: 0.5 g per 100 g

Serving Size: 1 clove (approx. 3 g)

Glycemic load (GL): Very low

Special Benefits: Garlic has numerous health benefits. It contains bioactive compounds such as allicin that act as powerful antioxidants and possess anti-inflammatory properties. Garlic can help lower blood sugar and improve insulin sensitivity, which is especially beneficial for diabetics. In addition, garlic has antimicrobial and heart-protective properties, which can lead to an overall improvement in cardiovascular health.

Recommended Preparation Methods: Garlic can be used raw, minced or pressed as a condiment. It is excellent for frying in oil, as an ingredient in soups, stews, dressings and marinades. Many chefs also add it to oven dishes or pasta sauces to enhance the flavor.

Ginger

Glycemic Index (GI): ~15 (low)

Carbohydrate content: 18 g per 100 g

Fibre content: 2 g per 100 g

Protein: 1.8 g per 100 g

Fat content: 0.8 g per 100 g

Serving Size: 1 teaspoon freshly grated (about 2 g)

Glycemic load (GL): Very low

Special Benefits: Ginger is known for its anti-inflammatory and antioxidant properties. It can help regulate blood sugar levels and improve insulin sensitivity. In addition, ginger has a digestive effect and can relieve nausea.

Recommended preparation methods: Freshly grated or sliced as an addition to tea, smoothies, soups or curries. Also included as a dried powder in spice blends or in pastries.

Ginger is a versatile and healthy spice that can be excellently integrated into the diet of people with type 2 diabetes. It can help keep blood sugar levels balanced while providing numerous health benefits.

Goat cheese (low fat)

Glycemic Index (GI): 0 (no effect on blood sugar levels)

Carbohydrate content: 1 g per 100 g

Fiber content: 0 g per 100 g

Protein: 20 g per 100 g

Fat content: 15 g per 100 g

Serving Size: 30 g (about 1 thin slice)

Glycemic load (GL): Very low

Special advantages:

- High protein content that has a satiating effect and supports muscle building.

- Contains less lactose than cow's milk products, which can be beneficial for people with lactose intolerance.

- Rich in calcium, which is important for healthy bones and teeth.

- Contains medium-chain fatty acids (MCFAs) that are easier to digest and can be converted into energy more quickly.

- Contains probiotic cultures that can promote gut health.

Recommended preparation methods:

- As a salad topping.

- On wholemeal bread or in sandwiches.

- In savory dishes such as quiches or frittatas.

- As a spread on vegetable sticks.

The low-fat goat cheese is an excellent choice for people with type 2 diabetes because it does not affect blood sugar levels, is satiating, and offers various health benefits.

Grapefruit

Glycemic Index (GI): 25 (low)

Carbohydrate content: 8.1 g per 100 g

Fibre content: 1.6 g per 100 g

Protein: 0.8 g per 100 g

Fat content: 0.1 g per 100 g

Serving Size: 1/2 medium grapefruit (approx. 123 g)

Glycemic load (GL): Very low

Special benefits: Rich in vitamins C, A and antioxidants that can strengthen the immune system and reduce cell damage. Additionally, grapefruit helps promote digestion and support a healthy cardiovascular system.

Recommended preparation methods: Fresh as a snack, in fruit salads or as a juice. Especially delicious in combination with other citrus fruits or in hearty salads for a refreshing, sour taste.

Note: Grapefruit may interact with certain medications. Consult your doctor if you are taking medication regularly.

Haws

Glycemic Index (GI): Unknown (typically very low due to high fiber content)

Carbohydrate content: Approx. 60 g per 100 g (dried)

Fiber content: Approx. 24 g per 100 g (dried)

Protein: Approx. 1.6 g per 100 g

Fat content: 0.3 g per 100 g

Serving Size: 1 tablespoon dried rose hips (about 5 g)

Glycemic Load (GL): Unknown (probably very low due to the small portion size and high fiber content)

Special advantages:

- Rich in fiber, which can support blood sugar control and aid digestion.

- Excellent source of vitamin C, which strengthens the immune system and has antioxidant properties.

- Contains vitamin A, which is good for skin and eye health.

- Contains secondary plant substances such as flavonoids, which can have an anti-inflammatory and antioxidant effect.

Recommended Preparation Methods: Dried rose hips can be made into rosehip tea, as an ingredient in fruit teas, powders can be mixed into smoothies, yogurt or cereal. Also popular as an ingredient in jams and jellies.

Hazelnuts

Glycemic Index (GI): 15 (low)

Carbohydrate content: 17 g per 100 g

Fibre content: 9.7 g per 100 g

Protein: 15 g per 100 g

Fat content: 61 g per 100 g (higher proportion of monounsaturated and polyunsaturated fatty acids)

Serving Size: About 30 g (about a handful)

Glycemic load (GL): Very low

Special advantages:

- High content of fiber, which can help improve digestion and increase satiety.

- Rich in vitamin E, which has antioxidant properties and can protect cells from damage.

- Good source of magnesium, which is important for blood sugar control and nerve function.

- Contains healthy fats, especially monounsaturated and polyunsaturated fatty acids, which may contribute to heart health.

- Possesses antioxidants such as phytosterols, which have anti-inflammatory properties.

Recommended preparation methods:

- As a snack, raw or roasted (without salt).

- Chopped or ground to refine salads, yoghurts or smoothies.

- In homemade nut butter.

- As an ingredient in baked goods, such as in wholemeal bread or muffins, where the added sugar should be controlled.

Hazelnuts are an excellent addition to the diet of people with type 2 diabetes because they have a very low glycemic index and a very low glycemic load. Their rich nutritional composition can help stabilize blood sugar levels and promote overall health.

Honeydew

Glycemic Index (GI): 65 (medium)

Carbohydrate content: 8 g per 100 g

Fiber content: 0.9 g per 100 g

Protein: 0.5 g per 100 g

Fat content: 0.1 g per 100 g

Serving Size: 1 cup diced (about 160 g)

Glycemic load (GL): Medium

Special advantages: High water content, provides important vitamins such as vitamin C and vitamin A, good source of electrolytes such as potassium and magnesium, which can be especially helpful during the hot summer months.

Recommended Preparation Methods: Fresh as a snack, in fruit salads, as an ingredient in smoothies or as a refreshing ingredient in savory dishes such as cold gazpacho soups or salads.

Note for type 2 diabetics: Since honeydew melons have a higher glycemic index, they should be consumed in moderation and preferably in combination with protein-rich and high-fiber foods to avoid a rapid increase in blood sugar levels.

Hummus (no added sugar)

Glycemic Index (GI): 6 (very low)

Carbohydrate content: 14.3 g per 100 g

Fibre content: 6.0 g per 100 g

Protein: 7.9 g per 100 g

Fat content: 9.6 g per 100 g

Serving Size: 2 tablespoons (about 30 g)

Glycemic load (GL): Very low

Special benefits: Hummus is an excellent source of vegetable protein and fiber, which can help with satiety. It also contains healthy fats that come from olive oil and sesame paste (tahini), which is good for the cardiovascular system. Hummus also contains various vitamins and minerals such as iron, magnesium, and B vitamins. Due to the fiber, hummus can help stabilize blood sugar levels, which is especially beneficial for people with type 2 diabetes.

Recommended ways to prepare hummus: Hummus can be used as a dip for vegetables or whole grains, as a spread for sandwiches or wraps, or as an accompaniment to various dishes such as roasted vegetables or salads.

Isoflavones (from soybeans)

Glycemic Index (GI): 14 (low)

Carbohydrate content: 9.9 g per 100 g

Fiber content: 6 g per 100 g

Protein: 36.5 g per 100 g

Fat content: 20 g per 100 g

Serving Size: 1/2 cup (about 90 g)

Glycemic load (GL): Very low

Special benefits: Isoflavones are a class of phytoestrogens found in soybeans. They are known for their antioxidant properties and their ability to reduce inflammation. Isoflavones can also help improve insulin sensitivity, thus helping to regulate blood sugar levels. In addition, they have potential protective effects against cardiovascular disease and osteoporosis.

Recommended preparation methods: Soybeans can be prepared in a variety of ways, such as tofu, tempeh, miso, or soy milk. They are also great as an addition to soups, salads or as an accompaniment to main courses.

Jackfruit

Glycemic Index (GI): 50 (medium)

Carbohydrate content: 23 g per 100 g

Fiber content: 1.5 g per 100 g

Protein: 1.7 g per 100 g

Fat content: 0.3 g per 100 g

Serving Size: 1 cup (about 165 g)

Glycemic load (GL): Medium

Special benefits: Jackfruit is rich in vitamin C, vitamin A, magnesium and potassium. It also contains antioxidants that can help fight free radicals. In addition, jackfruit can contribute to better digestion due to its high fiber content.

Recommended ways to prepare it: Jackfruit can be eaten raw, but it is also a popular ingredient in curries, chutneys and salads. It can be used as a meat substitute in savory dishes, especially in vegan and vegetarian recipes.

Jerusalem artichoke

Glycemic Index (GI): 50 (medium)

Carbohydrate content: 17 g per 100 g

Fibre content: 1.6 g per 100 g

Protein: 2 g per 100 g

Fat content: 0.01 g per 100 g

Serving Size: 1 cup cooked (about 150 g)

Glycemic load (GL): Medium

Special advantages:

- Rich in inulin, a fibre that reduces blood sugar levels and promotes intestinal health.

- Good source of potassium, iron, and vitamin B1.

- May help regulate blood sugar levels as it improves insulin sensitivity.

Recommended preparation methods:

- Steam or boil for easy, gentle preparation.

- Fry or bake for a more intense flavor.

- Can be used raw in salads to provide a crisp texture.

Jicama (Mexican yam)

Glycemic Index (GI): 15 (low)

Carbohydrate content: 9 g per 100 g

Fiber content: 5 g per 100 g

Protein: 1 g per 100 g

Fat content: 0.1 g per 100 g

Serving Size: 1 cup raw (about 130 g)

Glycemic load (GL): Very low

Special advantages:

Jicama is rich in fiber, especially inulin, a prebiotic fiber that can support gut health. It also contains vitamin C, which boosts the immune system, as well as potassium, which helps regulate blood pressure. This root tuber is also low in calories, making it a good choice for diabetics who want to control their weight.

Recommended preparation methods:

Jicama can be consumed raw in salads or as a healthy snack. It can also be used in vegetable stir-fries, soups or stews. Another popular method is cutting into sticks and seasoning with lime juice and chili for a refreshing and savory snack.

Kale

Glycemic Index (GI): 2 (very low)

Carbohydrate content: 8.8 g per 100 g

Fibre content: 2 g per 100 g

Protein: 4.3 g per 100 g

Fat content: 0.9 g per 100 g

Serving Size: 1 cup chopped (about 67 g)

Glycemic load (GL): Very low

Special benefits: Kale is extremely nutritious and an excellent source of vitamins A, C and K. In addition, it contains a good amount of calcium, iron and various antioxidants such as carotenoids and flavonoids, which can reduce the risk of chronic diseases. The high fiber content helps regulate blood sugar, which is especially beneficial for people with type 2 diabetes. Kale can also have anti-inflammatory effects and supports cardiovascular health.

Recommended ways to cook: Kale can be prepared in a variety of ways, including steaming, blanching, frying, or even eating raw in smoothies and salads. In order to preserve the nutrients optimally, steaming or raw consumption is often preferred.

Kalettes (kale-Brussels sprout hybrid)

Glycemic Index (GI): Not clearly shown, probably very low due to the low carbohydrate content.

Carbohydrate content: Approximately 3-4 g per 100 g (estimate based on similar green leafy vegetables)

Fiber content: Approximately 3-4 g per 100 g (estimate, since both kale and Brussels sprouts are high in fiber)

Protein: About 3 g per 100 g

Fat content: 0.5 g per 100 g

Serving Size: 1 cup (about 100-150 g)

Glycemic load (GL): Very low

Special Benefits: Kalettes combine the health benefits of kale and Brussels sprouts. They are rich in fiber, vitamins C and K, and antioxidants. These nutrients support the immune system, promote bone health, and can reduce inflammation.

Recommended ways of preparation: Steaming, bleaching, enjoying raw in salads or lightly sautéing, can also be used as a side dish or in stir-fries.

Kamut

Glycemic Index (GI): 45 (medium)

Carbohydrate content: 65 g per 100 g

Fiber content: 8 g per 100 g

Protein: 14 g per 100 g

Fat content: 2 g per 100 g

Serving Size: 1 cup cooked (about 160 g)

Glycemic load (GL): Medium

Special benefits: Kamut is an ancient grain rich in protein, fiber, and important minerals such as magnesium, zinc, and iron. It has a nutty flavor and provides more protein and nutrients than traditional wheat. Thanks to its low gluten content, it is often better tolerated than modern wheat varieties.

Recommended ways to prepare: Kamut can be cooked in a similar way to rice or quinoa. It is ideal for salads, as an accompaniment to main courses or as a base for cereal dishes. Kamut can also be processed into flour and used in baked goods.

Kiwano

Glycemic Index (GI): 40 (low)

Carbohydrate content: 8 g per 100 g

Fibre content: 2 g per 100 g

Protein: 1.8 g per 100 g

Fat content: 1.3 g per 100 g

Serving Size: 1 fruit (approx. 200 g)

Glycemic Load (GL): Low

Special benefits: Kiwano, also known as horned cucumber or African horned melon, is rich in fiber, vitamin C and various minerals such as magnesium and iron. It also contains antioxidants and has a high water content, which contributes to hydration.

Recommended ways to cook: Kiwano can be eaten raw by cutting the fruit in half and scooping out the jelly-like flesh with a spoon. It can also be used as an ingredient in fruit salads, smoothies or as a decoration for desserts.

Kiwi

Glycemic Index (GI): 50 (medium)

Carbohydrate content: 14 g per 100 g

Fibre content: 3 g per 100 g

Protein: 1.1 g per 100 g

Fat content: 0.5 g per 100 g

Serving Size: 1 piece (approx. 75 g)

Glycemic Load (GL): Low

Special benefits: Rich in fiber, vitamins C, E and K. Kiwifruit is also a good source of folic acid, potassium and antioxidants, which can help reduce oxidative stress. They can strengthen the immune system and promote digestion.

Recommended preparation methods: Consume fresh, in fruit salads, smoothies or as a topping for yoghurt.

The kiwifruit is an excellent choice for people with type 2 diabetes because it has a moderate GI but a low glycemic load. The high fiber content can help stabilize blood sugar levels and minimize the risk of blood sugar spikes. In addition to being delicious and refreshing, kiwifruit offers significant health benefits that go far beyond its low impact on blood sugar.

Kohlrabi

Glycemic Index (GI): 20 (low)

Carbohydrate content: 6.2 g per 100 g

Fiber content: 3.6 g per 100 g

Protein: 1.7 g per 100 g

Fat content: 0.1 g per 100 g

Serving Size: 1 cup chopped (about 135 g)

Glycemic load (GL): Very low

Special benefits: Kohlrabi is high in fiber, which aids digestion and helps control blood sugar. It is also an excellent source of vitamin C, which boosts the immune system and has anti-inflammatory properties. Additionally, kohlrabi contains vitamin B6, potassium, and magnesium, which contribute to overall health.

Recommended ways to prepare: Kohlrabi can be eaten raw in salads, which brings out the crunchy texture and slightly sweet taste. It is also great for steaming, frying, or as an ingredient in soups and stews. Kohlrabi can also be used in purees or sliced and served as a snack with a healthy dip.

Leaf spinach

Glycemic Index (GI): Very low (less than 15)

Carbohydrate content: 3.6 g per 100 g

Fiber content: 2.2 g per 100 g

Protein: 2.9 g per 100 g

Fat content: 0.4 g per 100 g

Serving Size: 1 cup cooked (about 180 g)

Glycemic load (GL): Very low

Special benefits: Spinach leaves are rich in vitamins A, C, and K, as well as folic acid, iron, and potassium. These nutrients are important for the immune system, blood health, and bone health. Additionally, spinach contains antioxidants such as lutein and zeaxanthin, which can help maintain eye health and reduce inflammation.

Recommended preparation methods: Steamed, lightly cooked or raw in salads. Spinach leaves can also be used in smoothies, soups, and as a side dish in various dishes.

Spinach leaves are an ideal food for type 2 diabetics, as it does not raise blood sugar much due to its low glycemic index and glycemic load. The high nutrient density and rich fiber content contribute to overall health and satiety, which is important for weight management.

Leek

Glycemic Index (GI): 15 (low)

Carbohydrate content: 14 g per 100 g

Fiber content: 1.8 g per 100 g

Protein: 1.5 g per 100 g

Fat content: 0.3 g per 100 g

Serving Size: 1 cup cooked (about 120 g)

Glycemic load (GL): Very low

Special benefits: Rich in vitamin K, vitamin A, and antioxidants that can help reduce inflammation. Contains prebiotics that support digestive health.

Recommended preparation methods: steaming, boiling, roasting or as an ingredient in soups and stews.

Lemon

Glycemic Index (GI): Unknown (usually classified as very low)

Carbohydrate content: 9 g per 100 g

Fiber content: 2.8 g per 100 g

Protein: 1.1 g per 100 g

Fat content: 0.3 g per 100 g

Serving Size: 1 medium lemon (approx. 58 g)

Glycemic load (GL): Very low

Special benefits: Lemons are rich in vitamin C, which can strengthen the immune system. They also contain flavonoids, which have antioxidant and anti-inflammatory properties. Due to their high fiber content, they can promote digestion and help regulate blood sugar levels.

Recommended Ways to Brew: Lemon juice can be used in water, teas, or smoothies to enhance flavor and provide additional nutrients. Lemon peel can be used in dishes as an aromatic ingredient. In addition, lemons can serve as a marinade for fish or meat or be used in salad dressings and sauces.

Overall, lemons are a versatile and healthy addition to a balanced diet, especially for people with type 2 diabetes, as they have low amounts of carbohydrates and do not greatly affect blood sugar levels.

Lentils (brown, red, green)

Glycemic Index (GI): 22-30 (low)

Carbohydrate content: 20 g per 100 g

Fiber content: 8 g per 100 g

Protein: 9 g per 100 g

Fat content: 0.4 g per 100 g

Serving Size: 1 cup cooked (about 198 g)

Glycemic Load (GL): Low

Special benefits: Lentils are an excellent source of vegetable protein and fiber. They contain important nutrients such as iron, folic acid, potassium and magnesium. They also promote heart health, stabilize blood sugar levels, and aid digestion.

Recommended preparation methods: Cooking, as a base for soups, stews or salads, processed into lentil patties and dips.

Lima beans

Glycemic Index (GI): 32 (low)

Carbohydrate content: 20 g per 100 g

Fibre content: 7 g per 100 g

Protein: 7 g per 100 g

Fat content: 0.4 g per 100 g

Serving Size: 1/2 cup cooked (about 85 g)

Glycemic Load (GL): Low

Special benefits: Lima beans are an excellent source of fiber and protein, making them a nutritious supplement for diabetics. They also contain important vitamins and minerals such as iron, magnesium, potassium and vitamin B6. Also, the fiber in lima beans can help regulate blood sugar levels and promote digestive health.

Recommended Preparation Methods: Lima beans can be boiled, steamed, or used in soups, stews, and salads. They also go well as an accompaniment to meat and fish dishes. Be sure to rinse lima beans thoroughly before cooking and cook enough to facilitate digestion and remove any anti-nutritional agents.

Limes

Glycemic Index (GI): 0 (very low)

Carbohydrate content: 11 g per 100 g

Fiber content: 2.8 g per 100 g

Protein: 0.7 g per 100 g

Fat content: 0.2 g per 100 g

Serving Size: 1 lime (approx. 67 g)

Glycemic load (GL): Very low

Special benefits: Limes are extremely low in calories and contain a high concentration of vitamin C, which strengthens the immune system. They are also rich in antioxidants that help fight free radicals and protect the body from oxidative stress. The acidic juices and peel oils of limes have anti-inflammatory properties and aid digestion. In addition, lime juice has an alcalizing effect and can help to balance the body's pH value.

Recommended preparation methods:

- Freshly squeezed juice as an ingredient for drinks or salad dressings

- As a flavouring agent in dishes such as fish, meat and vegetables

- In sauces and marinades

Limes are especially beneficial for people with type 2 diabetes because they don't raise blood sugar levels while still providing important nutrients and vitamins.

Low-fat quark

Glycemic index (GI): approx. 30 (low)

Carbohydrate content: 4 g per 100 g

Fiber content: 0 g per 100 g

Protein: 12 g per 100 g

Fat content: 0.2 g per 100 g

Serving Size: 1 cup (about 250 g)

Glycemic load (GL): Very low

Special benefits: Low-fat quark is an excellent source of protein that helps keep blood sugar levels stable. In addition, it is rich in calcium and vitamin B12, which is essential for bone health and the formation of red blood cells. Low-fat quark is also low in fat and calories, making it a good choice for a calorie-conscious diet.

Recommended preparation methods: Low-fat quark can be enjoyed on its own or used as a base for desserts and dips. It is ideal for smoothies, as a spread on wholemeal bread, or as a topping for fruit salads and muesli.

Lupin flour

Glycemic Index (GI): 15 (low)

Carbohydrate content: 11.5 g per 100 g

Fibre content: 30 g per 100 g

Protein: 40 g per 100 g

Fat content: 7 g per 100 g

Serving Size: 1 tablespoon (about 10 g)

Glycemic load (GL): Very low

Special advantages: Lupin flour is particularly rich in fiber and protein. It contains all the essential amino acids, making it an excellent source of vegetable protein. In addition, it has a low carbohydrate content, which makes it especially beneficial for people with type 2 diabetes. It also contains important vitamins and minerals such as vitamin E, magnesium and calcium. Lupin flour also has antioxidant properties that can help prevent cell damage and reduce inflammation.

Recommended preparation methods: Lupin flour can be used in a variety of ways in the kitchen. It's great to add to baked goods like bread, muffins, or pancakes to increase protein and fiber content. It can also be used in smoothies or as a thickener for soups and sauces. It can also be used in part as a substitute for other types of flour in recipes to improve nutritional value.

Macadamia nuts

Glycemic Index (GI): Very low

Carbohydrate content: 4 g per 100 g

Fibre content: 8.6 g per 100 g

Protein: 7.9 g per 100 g

Fat content: 76 g per 100 g

Serving Size: One handful (about 28 g)

Glycemic load (GL): Very low

Special benefits: Macadamia nuts are rich in healthy fats, especially monounsaturated fatty acids, which are good for the heart. They also contain fiber, which contributes to better digestion, and are a source of vitamins and minerals such as vitamin B1 (thiamine), magnesium, and iron. The antioxidant properties of nuts can help stabilize blood sugar levels and reduce inflammation.

Recommended ways to prepare: Best in moderation as a healthy snack, raw or roasted. They can also be chopped and used in salads, yogurt, cereals, or as a special extra in baked goods.

Mangoes (in moderation)

Glycemic Index (GI): 51 (medium)

Carbohydrate content: 15 g per 100 g

Fibre content: 1.6 g per 100 g

Protein: 0.8 g per 100 g

Fat content: 0.4 g per 100 g

Serving Size: 1/2 cup sliced (about 83 g)

Glycemic load (GL): Medium

Special benefits: Mangoes are rich in vitamin C, vitamin A and folic acid. They also contain antioxidants such as mangiferin, which may have anti-inflammatory and anti-diabetic properties. Mangoes offer a variety of health benefits, including supporting the immune system and improving digestion.

Recommended ways of preparation: In moderation as a snack, in fruit salads or smoothies. Mangoes should be consumed in a controlled manner for type 2 diabetes to avoid blood sugar spikes. A combination with high-fat or high-fiber foods can further reduce glycemic load.

Millet

Glycemic Index (GI): 71 (medium)

Carbohydrate content: 73 g per 100 g

Fiber content: 8.5 g per 100 g

Protein: 11 g per 100 g

Fat content: 4.2 g per 100 g

Serving Size: 1 cup cooked (about 174 g)

Glycemic load (GL): Medium

Special benefits: Millet is gluten-free and rich in fiber, magnesium, iron and antioxidants. It supports digestion and can protect the cardiovascular system. Millet has a low fat content but a high percentage of vegetable protein, which makes it a valuable addition to a balanced diet.

Recommended preparation methods: Boil and serve as a side dish, in salads, as porridge or in the form of millet flakes in muesli.

Millet can be a healthy and nutritious supplement for type 2 diabetics, but it should be enjoyed in moderation as it has a medium glycemic index.

Miso

Glycemic Index (GI): Unknown (very low estimate)

Carbohydrate content: 27 g per 100 g

Fibre content: 5.4 g per 100 g

Protein: 12 g per 100 g

Fat content: 6 g per 100 g

Serving Size: 1 tbsp (approx. 18 g)

Glycemic load (GL): Very low

Special benefits: Miso is a fermented soy paste that is rich in probiotics and can help improve digestion. It also contains essential amino acids, various B vitamins, vitamin K, and numerous minerals such as zinc, copper, and manganese. Because it is fermented, it can help stabilize blood sugar levels and boost the immune system.

Recommended ways to prepare it: Miso can be used in soups, dressings, or marinades. It's important not to overheat miso as this can destroy the beneficial probiotics. When miso is used as a paste, it should be dissolved in warm but not boiling hot liquids to maximize its health benefits.

Mountain lentils

Glycemic Index (GI): 21 (low)

Carbohydrate content: 20 g per 100 g

Fiber content: 8 g per 100 g

Protein: 9 g per 100 g

Fat content: 0.5 g per 100 g

Serving Size: 1 cup cooked (about 200 g)

Glycemic Load (GL): Low to medium, depending on serving size

Special Benefits: Mountain lentils are rich in fiber and plant-based protein, making them an excellent choice for blood sugar control. The high fiber gain helps keep blood sugar stable and promote digestion. In addition, they are a good source of important micronutrients such as iron, magnesium, and B vitamins, which contribute to overall health.

Recommended preparation methods:

- Cook and serve as a side dish

- Use in soups and stews

- Use as a base for salads or plant-based burgers

Additionally, mountain lentils combined with whole grains can provide a complete source of protein and ensure a healthy and nutritious meal.

Mung beans

Glycemic Index (GI): 25 (low)

Carbohydrate content: 19 g per 100 g

Fiber content: 7.6 g per 100 g

Protein: 7 g per 100 g

Fat content: 0.4 g per 100 g

Serving Size: 1/2 cup cooked (about 100 g)

Glycemic Load (GL): Low

Special benefits: Mung beans are rich in fiber, which can promote digestion and stabilize blood sugar levels. They also contain a significant amount of plant-based protein, making them an excellent source of protein for vegetarians and vegans. In addition, they are rich in vitamins and minerals such as iron, magnesium, potassium and vitamin B6. Mung beans also contain antioxidants and anti-inflammatory compounds that may contribute to overall health.

Recommended ways to prepare them: Mung beans can be used in a variety of dishes. They are great for soups, stews, salads and can also be used cooked and pureed as a base for dips or spreads. They can also be sprouted and eaten raw in salads or as a side dish.

Nashi pear

Glycemic Index (GI): 32 (low)

Carbohydrate content: 13 g per 100 g

Fibre content: 3 g per 100 g

Protein: 0.5 g per 100 g

Fat content: 0.2 g per 100 g

Serving Size: 1 medium Nashi pear (about 150 g)

Glycemic Load (GL): Low

Special Benefits: Nashi pears are high in fiber, which aids digestion and promotes blood sugar control. They also contain vitamin C, potassium and small amounts of vitamin K and copper. The pears are also hydrating because they have a high water content.

Recommended preparation methods: Fresh as a snack, in salads, or lightly steamed. They can also be used in smoothies or desserts.

Nectarines

Glycemic Index (GI): 43 (low-medium)

Carbohydrate content: 8 g per 100 g

Fiber content: 1.7 g per 100 g

Protein: 1 g per 100 g

Fat content: 0.1 g per 100 g

Serving Size: 1 medium fruit (approx. 150 g)

Glycemic Load (GL): Low

Special benefits: Nectarines are rich in fiber, vitamins A and C, and potassium. They contain antioxidants such as beta-carotene, which can help improve skin health and support the immune system.

Recommended preparation methods: Fresh as a snack, in fruit salads, as an ingredient in smoothies or as a topping for yoghurt and oatmeal. Nectarines can also be lightly grilled to caramelize their natural sugars and add an extra level of flavor.

Nettle

Glycemic Index (GI): Unknown (probably very low)

Carbohydrate content: About 7 g per 100 g

Fiber content: About 6.9 g per 100 g

Protein: About 4 g per 100 g

Fat content: About 0.2 g per 100 g

Serving Size: 1 cup cooked (about 150 g)

Glycemic load (GL): Very low

Special benefits: Nettles are rich in vitamins A, C, K and several B vitamins. They also contain numerous minerals such as iron, magnesium, calcium and phosphorus. They also offer a high amount of antioxidants, which can help reduce inflammation and strengthen the immune system. In addition, they are known for their diuretic properties, which can be helpful in detoxifying the body.

Recommended ways of preparation: Nettles can be boiled, steamed or added to smoothies. They are also great for soups and teas. Before preparation, the burning hairs should be removed by blanching or drying.

Nutmeg

Glycemic Index (GI): Very low (below 5)

Carbohydrate content: 28 g per 100 g

Fibre content: 20 g per 100 g

Protein: 6 g per 100 g

Fat content: 36 g per 100 g

Serving size: In recipes and dishes, it is often used in much smaller amounts, typically in knife tips or pinches.

Glycemic load (GL): Very low due to the small quantities used

Special benefits: Rich in fiber, which can help regulate blood sugar levels.

- Contains essential oils such as myristicin, elemicin, eugenol, and safrol, which may have anti-inflammatory properties.

- Known for its antioxidant properties.

- May aid digestion and relieve flatulence.

Recommended Preparation Methods: Nutmeg is mostly used as a spice in small amounts in various foods and drinks. It is great for seasoning:

- Vegetable dishes

- Soups and stews

- Sauces and dressings

- Baked goods such as cakes and biscuits

- Hot drinks such as tea or mulled wine

Important note:

Nutmeg should only be consumed in small quantities, as toxic effects can occur if consumed in excess.

Nuts (mixed, natural)

Glycemic Index (GI): 15-25 (low)

Carbohydrate content: 9-24 g per 100 g (depending on the type of nut)

Fiber content: 7-10 g per 100 g (depending on the type of nut)

Protein: 15-25 g per 100 g (depending on the type of nut)

Fat content: 45-65 g per 100 g (mainly healthy fats)

Serving Size: 28 g (about a handful)

Glycemic load (GL): Very low

Special advantages:

- Rich in healthy unsaturated fats that can have a positive effect on the cardiovascular system.

- High fiber content, which promotes digestion and ensures a longer feeling of satiety.

- Good source of vegetable protein.

- Contains important micronutrients such as vitamin E, magnesium, potassium and zinc.

- Natural source of antioxidants.

Recommended preparation methods:

- Pure as a snack.

- In salads or as a topping for dishes.

- Mixed into yogurts or smoothies.

- In homemade muesli bars or granola.

Important note:

Natural, unsalted nuts are preferable to avoid additional salt and sugar consumption. Since nuts are high in calories, the portion size should be considered.

Oat bran

Glycemic Index (GI): 55 (medium range)

Carbohydrate content: 58 g per 100 g

Fibre content: 15 g per 100 g

Protein: 17 g per 100 g

Fat content: 7 g per 100 g

Serving Size: 1/3 cup (about 20 g)

Glycemic Load (GL): Medium to low, depending on serving size

Special benefits: Oat bran is particularly rich in soluble fiber, especially beta-glucan, which has been shown to stabilize blood sugar levels and lower cholesterol levels. It also contains a good amount of protein and iron, as well as other micronutrients such as magnesium and zinc. The high fiber content promotes digestive health and can increase satiety, which can be helpful in weight management.

Recommended Preparation Methods: Oat bran can be mixed raw into smoothies or yogurt, used as an ingredient in baked goods such as muffins and bread, or cooked into porridge. It is also suitable as a topping for soups and salads.

Oatmeal

Glycemic Index (GI): 55 (medium range)

Carbohydrate content: 66 g per 100 g

Fibre content: 10 g per 100 g

Protein: 13 g per 100 g

Fat content: 7 g per 100 g

Serving Size: 1/2 cup (about 40 g, uncooked)

Glycemic Load (GL): Medium to high (depending on serving size)

Special advantages:

- Rich in soluble fiber, especially beta-glucan, which can help stabilize blood sugar levels and lower LDL cholesterol.

- Good source of important minerals such as manganese, phosphorus, magnesium and zinc.

- Contains a moderate amount of vegetable protein.

- Supports intestinal health due to the fiber it contains and promotes a long-lasting feeling of satiety.

Recommended preparation methods:

- Classic as a warm breakfast of porridge with water or milk (plant-based milk options also possible).

- As a base for overnight oats (oatmeal soaked overnight), combined with yoghurt, fruit and nuts.

- In smoothies for an extra portion of fiber and nutrients.

- For making homemade muesli or granola, with nuts, seeds and dried fruits.

- In baked goods such as health-promoting biscuits or energy bars.

Hint:

- When choosing oatmeal, it is advisable to bet on products that are as unprocessed as possible, such as whole oatmeal or coarsely chopped oats, as instant oatmeal can have a higher GI.

- Oatmeal can be problematic for people with gluten sensitivity if it has been contaminated during processing. Care should be taken of products certified gluten-free if this is a potential problem.

Okra

Glycemic Index (GI): 20 (low)

Carbohydrate content: 7.03 g per 100 g

Fibre content: 3.2 g per 100 g

Protein: 1.9 g per 100 g

Fat content: 0.2 g per 100 g

Serving Size: 1 cup sliced, cooked (about 180 g)

Glycemic load (GL): Very low

Special benefits: Okra is rich in fiber, which can help regulate blood sugar levels. It also contains a variety of vitamins and minerals, including vitamin C, vitamin K, folate, and magnesium. In addition, okra has antioxidant properties and can have an anti-inflammatory effect.

Recommended ways to prepare it: Okra can be prepared by steaming, boiling, or braising. It is great for soups, stews and as a side dish. Okra is also a delicious and healthy option when pan-fried, for example with a little olive oil and spices.

Olive oil

Glycemic Index (GI): 0 (low)

Carbohydrate content: 0 g per 100 g

Fiber content: 0 g per 100 g

Protein: 0 g per 100 g

Fat content: 100 g per 100 g

Serving Size: 1 tablespoon (about 13.5 g)

Glycemic load (GL): Very low

Special advantages:

- Olive oil is rich in monounsaturated fatty acids, especially oleic acid, which has been linked to improved heart health.

- It contains antioxidants such as vitamin E and polyphenols, which can reduce inflammation and help prevent chronic diseases.

- Research suggests that regular consumption of olive oil can stabilize blood sugar levels and improve insulin sensitivity.

- The inclusion of olive oil in the diet can thus contribute to the prevention of cardiovascular diseases, which often pose a higher risk in diabetics.

Recommended preparation methods:

- As a dressing for salads and raw vegetables

- For steaming vegetables

- For refining wholemeal bread or as a dip

- In sauces and marinades

Olive oil should preferably be used in its virgin, cold-pressed form (extra virgin), as this offers the highest quality and most health benefits. When heating olive oil, care should be taken not to heat it beyond the smoke points so as not to destroy the valuable nutrients.

Olives

Glycemic Index (GI): Very low

Carbohydrate content: Approx. 3.1 g per 100 g

Fiber content: Approx. 3.3 g per 100 g

Protein: Approx. 0.8 g per 100 g

Fat content: Approx. 15 g per 100 g

Serving Size: 1 tablespoon (about 8 g)

Glycemic load (GL): Very low

Special advantages:

- **Healthy fats:** Olives have a high content of monounsaturated fatty acids, especially oleic acid, which can promote heart health.

- **Antioxidants:** They contain polyphenols and vitamin E, which have antioxidant properties and can help reduce cell damage.

- **Anti-inflammatory:** The ingredients in olives can help reduce inflammation and thus prevent chronic diseases.

- **Blood sugar control:** Due to the low glycemic index, olives are great for diabetics, as they have minimal effect on blood sugar.

Recommended preparation methods:

- **As a snack:** Straight from the package or jar.

- **In salads:** To add to various salads for extra flavor and nutritional value.

- **Cooked dishes:** Part of tapas, pasta, pizza, or other Mediterranean dishes.

- **On bread or crackers:** Sliced or as a paste (such as olive tapenade).

Olives are not only diverse in taste, but also a nutrient-rich addition to the diet of type 2 diabetics.

Onions

Glycemic Index (GI): 10 (low)

Carbohydrate content: 9 g per 100 g

Fiber content: 1.7 g per 100 g

Protein: 1.1 g per 100 g

Fat content: 0.1 g per 100 g

Serving Size: 1 medium onion (approx. 110 g)

Glycemic load (GL): Very low

Special benefits: Onions are rich in antioxidants, especially quercetin, which has anti-inflammatory properties. They contain compounds such as sulfur, which can help lower blood sugar levels. In addition, onions are a good source of vitamin C and B vitamins, especially folate.

Recommended Preparation Methods: Onions can be enjoyed raw in salads or sandwiches, sautéed, fried, boiled, or used as an ingredient in soups, stews, and sauces. They add flavor and depth to dishes without many extra calories or carbohydrates.

Oranges

Glycemic Index (GI): 40-45 (low)

Carbohydrate content: 12 g per 100 g

Fibre content: 2.4 g per 100 g

Protein: 0.9 g per 100 g

Fat content: 0.1 g per 100 g

Serving Size: 1 medium orange (approx. 130 g)

Glycemic Load (GL): Low to moderate

Special benefits: Oranges are rich in vitamin C, which boosts the immune system, as well as fiber, which helps regulate blood sugar levels. They also contain flavonoids, which have anti-inflammatory effects and antioxidant properties. In addition, oranges support the maintenance of heart health and can promote digestion.

Recommended ways to prepare: Straight from hand as a snack, in fruit salads, as fresh orange juice (be careful not to add sugar) or as an addition to savory dishes such as chicken or fish for a fruity touch.

Pak Choi

Glycemic Index (GI): 15 (low)

Carbohydrate content: 1.2 g per 100 g

Fibre content: 1 g per 100 g

Protein: 1.5 g per 100 g

Fat content: 0.2 g per 100 g

Serving Size: 1 cup (about 170 g)

Glycemic load (GL): Very low

Special benefits: Pak choi is rich in vitamins C and K, as well as beta-carotene and folic acid. It contains antioxidants and minerals such as calcium, potassium and magnesium, which contribute to overall health and well-being. The antioxidants it contains can help reduce inflammation and strengthen the immune system.

Recommended ways to prepare it: Pak choi can be prepared in a variety of ways, such as steaming, sautéing, or as an ingredient in soups and salads. Because it cooks quickly, it's also great for stir-fries.

Pak choi, also known as Chinese collard greens, is a particularly nutrient-dense vegetable that is great for a healthy diet, especially for people with type 2 diabetes. Due to its low glycemic index and low glycemic load, pak choi does little to increase blood sugar levels and thus can help to better control blood sugar.

Papaya

Glycemic Index (GI): 60 (medium)

Carbohydrate content: 11 g per 100 g

Fiber content: 1.8 g per 100 g

Protein: 0.4 g per 100 g

Fat content: 0.1 g per 100 g

Serving Size: 1 cup diced (about 140 g)

Glycemic load (GL): Medium

Special advantages:

Papaya is an excellent source of vitamins C and A, both of which are powerful antioxidants and support the immune system. It also contains folic acid and potassium. The enzyme papain, which is found in papaya, can aid digestion and reduce inflammation. In addition, papaya contains carotenoids such as beta-carotene, which can promote heart health.

Recommended preparation methods:

Papaya can be eaten fresh, either on its own or as part of a fruit salad. It can also be blended into smoothies or used in savory dishes such as salsas and salads. Be sure to choose ripe fruits, as they are sweeter and more nutritious.

Paprika

Glycemic Index (GI): 10 (low)

Carbohydrate content: 6 g per 100 g

Fibre content: 2 g per 100 g

Protein: 1 g per 100 g

Fat content: 0.3 g per 100 g

Serving Size: 1 cup chopped (about 150 g)

Glycemic load (GL): Very low

Special benefits: Peppers, also known as sweet peppers, are rich in vitamins A and C and also contain a good amount of vitamin B6 and folate. These nutrients support immune function, eye health, and overall inflammation reduction. Peppers are also an excellent source of antioxidants such as beta-carotene and lutein, which help protect cells.

Recommended ways to prepare peppers: Peppers can be used raw in salads, as a snack with a healthy dip, grilled, stuffed, or in stir-fries. They can also be easily integrated into soups and stews or simply contribute to a mixed vegetable dish.

Parsley

Glycemic Index (GI): 5 (very low)

Carbohydrate content: 6 g per 100 g

Fibre content: 3.3 g per 100 g

Protein: 3 g per 100 g

Fat content: 0.8 g per 100 g

Serving Size: 1/2 cup freshly chopped (about 30 g)

Glycemic load (GL): Very low

Special benefits: Parsley is extremely nutritious and contains high amounts of vitamins A, C and K. It possesses anti-inflammatory and antioxidant properties that can help reduce inflammation. It is also said to have diuretic qualities that can help detoxify the body.

Recommended preparation methods: It can be used raw as a garnish or in salads, but also as an ingredient in soups, stews, smoothies or sauces.

Parsley offers a variety of health benefits and is an excellent choice for people with type 2 diabetes due to its very low glycemic index and low glycemic load. It helps to keep blood sugar levels stable and can be integrated into the daily diet in a variety of ways.

Parsnips

Glycemic Index (GI): About 52 (medium)

Carbohydrate content: 17.99 g per 100 g

Fibre content: 4.9 g per 100 g

Protein: 1.2 g per 100 g

Fat content: 0.3 g per 100 g

Serving Size: 1 cup, raw, sliced (about 133 g)

Glycemic load (GL): Medium

Special benefits: Parsnips are an excellent source of fiber, which can aid digestion and help with satiety. They are also rich in vitamins and minerals, especially vitamin C, vitamin K, and folic acid. Parsnips also contain a variety of antioxidants that can help reduce inflammation and boost the immune system. Due to their moderate GI value, they are a better substitute for high GI foods, such as potatoes, especially when kept in a balanced and controlled amount.

Recommended ways of preparation: Parsnips can be prepared in a variety of ways. They can be roasted, boiled, steamed or pureed. Parsnips can also be used raw in salads or as an ingredient in soups and stews. Roasting parsnips brings out their natural sweetness and can make them a delicious and healthy side dish.

Passion fruit

Glycemic Index (GI): 30 (low)

Carbohydrate content: 23.38 g per 100 g

Fiber content: 10.4 g per 100 g

Protein: 2.2 g per 100 g

Fat content: 0.4 g per 100 g

Serving Size: 1 cup (about 236 g)

Glycemic Load (GL): Low

Special benefits: Passion fruit is rich in fiber, vitamins C and A. It also contains important antioxidants such as beta-carotene and polyphenols, which can help boost the immune system and prevent chronic diseases. In addition, its fiber content can help improve digestion and stabilize blood sugar levels.

Recommended ways to prepare it: Passion fruit can be eaten fresh by scooping out the pulp. It is also excellent as an ingredient in smoothies, yoghurts, salads, desserts or as a topping for other dishes. If you like it exotic, you can make passion fruit juice or use the fruit as a base for sauces and dressings.

Peaches

Glycemic Index (GI): 42 (low-medium)

Carbohydrate content: 10 g per 100 g

Fiber content: 1.5 g per 100 g

Protein: 0.9 g per 100 g

Fat content: 0.1 g per 100 g

Serving Size: 1 medium peach (approx. 150 g)

Glycemic Load (GL): Low

Special benefits: Rich in vitamin C, vitamin A, and potassium; contains antioxidants that can support the immune system and reduce inflammation.

Recommended preparation methods: Fresh as a snack, in salads, in smoothies or grilled as a dessert.

Peaches are an excellent choice for people with type 2 diabetes because they not only contain a moderate amount of carbohydrates, but also provide many important nutrients. Their low to medium glycemic index means that they affect blood sugar levels only slowly and moderately, which helps them maintain their blood sugar control. The fiber it contains also helps to promote digestion and stabilize blood sugar levels.

Peanut butter (unsweetened)

Glycemic Index (GI): 14 (low)

Carbohydrate content: 20 g per 100 g

Fibre content: 6.0 g per 100 g

Protein: 25 g per 100 g

Fat content: 50 g per 100 g

Serving Size: 2 tablespoons (about 32 g)

Glycemic load (GL): Low (with moderate consumption)

Special benefits: Rich in healthy fats, especially monounsaturated and polyunsaturated fatty acids, contains good amounts of protein and fiber, which contributes to a longer-lasting feeling of satiety. Contains important vitamins and minerals such as vitamin E, magnesium and niacin. Can help keep blood sugar levels stable and is a good source of energy.

Recommended preparation methods: As a spread on wholemeal bread or crackers, as an ingredient in smoothies, dressings, or for dipping vegetable sticks.

Peanuts (unsalted)

Glycemic Index (GI): 14 (very low)

Carbohydrate content: 16 g per 100 g

Fiber content: 8.5 g per 100 g

Protein: 25.8 g per 100 g

Fat content: 49.2 g per 100 g

Serving Size: 1/4 cup (about 35 g)

Glycemic load (GL): Very low

Special advantages:

Peanuts are rich in healthy fats, proteins, and fiber. They are an excellent source of monounsaturated and polyunsaturated fatty acids, which are beneficial for heart health. In addition, peanuts contain important vitamins and minerals such as vitamin E, magnesium, and niacin, as well as antioxidants that can fight free radicals in the body. Peanuts can help increase satiety and keep blood sugar levels stable.

Recommended preparation methods:

Peanuts can be eaten raw, roasted, or used as an ingredient in various dishes such as salads and curries. They are also great as a snack in between meals if enjoyed in moderation. In addition, they can be made into peanut butter and used on bread or as a dip.

Hint:

Although peanuts offer many health benefits, diabetics should pay attention to serving size because they are high in calories. It is also important to prefer unsalted peanuts to minimize salt consumption.

Pears

Glycemic Index (GI): 38 (low to medium)

Carbohydrate content: 15 g per 100 g

Fibre content: 3.1 g per 100 g

Protein: 0.4 g per 100 g

Fat content: 0.1 g per 100 g

Serving Size: 1 medium pear (about 178 g)

Glycemic Load (GL): Low to Medium

Special benefits: Pears are high in fiber, especially soluble fiber, which can help regulate blood sugar levels and improve digestion. They also contain a variety of vitamins and minerals such as vitamin C, vitamin K, and potassium, as well as antioxidants that can fight cell damage.

Recommended preparation methods: Fresh as a snack, in salads, as a side dish in savory dishes, or lightly steamed or baked as a dessert.

Peas (green, yellow)

Glycemic Index (GI): 22 (low)

Carbohydrate content: 14 g per 100 g

Fiber content: 5 g per 100 g

Protein: 5 g per 100 g

Fat content: 0.4 g per 100 g

Serving Size: 1 cup cooked (about 160 g)

Glycemic Load (GL): Low

Special advantages:

Peas are high in fiber and protein, making them an excellent choice for type 2 diabetics. They also contain a good amount of vitamins such as vitamin A, vitamin K and vitamin C, as well as minerals such as iron and magnesium. The fiber helps regulate blood sugar levels and promotes healthy digestion. In addition, peas contain secondary plant substances that have an anti-inflammatory effect and can strengthen the immune system.

Recommended preparation methods:

Peas can be enjoyed in different ways: steamed, boiled, as a side dish in soups and stews, pureed as a dip or raw in salads. They go well with different flavors and are versatile in the kitchen.

Pecan nuts

Glycemic Index (GI): Very low (below 20)

Carbohydrate content: 4 g per 100 g

Fibre content: 9.6 g per 100 g

Protein: 9.2 g per 100 g

Fat content: 72 g per 100 g

Serving Size: 1 ounce (28 g) (about 19 half nuts)

Glycemic load (GL): Very low

Special advantages:

Pecans are particularly rich in monounsaturated fatty acids, which may contribute to heart health. They are also a good source of fiber, protein, as well as important vitamins and minerals such as vitamin E, magnesium and zinc. In addition, they contain antioxidants that have anti-inflammatory effects and can promote cellular health.

Recommended preparation methods:

- As a snack (raw or roasted)

- In salads for a crunchy effect

- Incorporated into baked goods (e.g. bread or muffins)

- Commonly used in healthy dessert recipes (e.g., as a topping for yogurt or grain bars)

Pecans are a tasty and nutritious option for people with type 2 diabetes, as their high fiber and fat content can help keep blood sugar stable and maintain satiety for longer. In moderate amounts, they are an excellent addition to a balanced diet.

Peppermint

Glycemic Index (GI): 0 (no carbohydrates)

Carbohydrate content: 0 g per 100 g

Fiber content: 0 g per 100 g

Protein: 3.8 g per 100 g

Fat content: 0.9 g per 100 g

Serving Size: 1 tablespoon fresh (approx. 2 g) or 1 tea bag (approx. 1 g)

Glycemic load (GL): Not applicable (as it does not contain carbohydrates)

Special benefits: Peppermint is known for its digestive properties. It can relieve symptoms such as flatulence, nausea and irritable bowel syndrome. In addition, it has antioxidant and anti-inflammatory properties that can contribute to overall health. Peppermint can also help regulate blood sugar levels, which can be especially beneficial for diabetics.

Recommended preparation methods: Fresh as a garnish for food, as an ingredient in salads or smoothies, infused as a tea or used as an essential oil.

Pineapple

Glycemic Index (GI): 66 (medium)

Carbohydrate content: 13 g per 100 g

Fibre content: 1.4 g per 100 g

Protein: 0.5 g per 100 g

Fat content: 0.1 g per 100 g

Serving Size: 1 cup (about 165 g)

Glycemic load (GL): Medium

Special benefits: Pineapple is rich in vitamin C, manganese and contains the enzyme bromelain, which has anti-inflammatory properties and can promote digestion. Pineapple also has antioxidant properties.

Recommended Preparation Methods: Fresh as a snack, in fruit salads, smoothies or as an ingredient in savory dishes such as curry and grilled vegetables.

Note: Due to the higher GI and carbohydrate content, diabetics should keep an eye on serving size and enjoy pineapple in moderation, combined with foods rich in protein and fiber to keep blood sugar levels stable.

Pistachios

Glycemic Index (GI): 15 (low)

Carbohydrate content: 28 g per 100 g

Fibre content: 10 g per 100 g

Protein: 20 g per 100 g

Fat content: 45 g per 100 g

Serving Size: 30 g (about a handful)

Glycemic Load (GL): Low

Special benefits: Pistachios are rich in healthy fats, protein, and fiber, making them a filling snack. They also contain important nutrients such as vitamin B6, thiamine (vitamin B1), copper and manganese. Pistachios also provide antioxidants and can have blood sugar-lowering effects because they help keep blood sugar levels stable.

Recommended preparation methods: Raw or roasted as a snack, chopped in salads or yogurt, or processed into baked goods. Be sure to choose unsalted varieties to keep sodium levels low.

Plums

Glycemic Index (GI): 29 (low)

Carbohydrate content: 11.4 g per 100 g

Fibre content: 1.4 g per 100 g

Protein: 0.7 g per 100 g

Fat content: 0.3 g per 100 g

Serving Size: 1 medium plum (about 65 g)

Glycemic Load (GL): Low

Special benefits: Prunes are rich in vitamins such as vitamins C, K and A, as well as important minerals such as potassium. They also contain antioxidants and polyphenols, which can help reduce inflammation. The fiber contained in plums can aid digestion and have a positive effect on blood sugar levels.

Recommended preparation methods: Fresh as a snack, added to salads, mixed into yogurt or smoothies, or as an ingredient in hot dishes such as stews or fruit compotes. Dried plums (prunes) are also a nutritious choice, although they have a higher sugar content and should be enjoyed in moderation.

Prunes can be a tasty and healthy addition to the diet plan of type 2 diabetics when enjoyed in appropriate amounts.

Pomegranate

Glycemic Index (GI): 35 (low)

Carbohydrate content: 19 g per 100 g

Fibre content: 4 g per 100 g

Protein: 1.7 g per 100 g

Fat content: 1.2 g per 100 g

Serving Size: 1/2 cup seeds (about 87 g)

Glycemic Load (GL): Low

Special benefits: Pomegranate seeds are rich in antioxidants, especially polyphenols, which can help reduce inflammatory processes. They are also a good source of vitamins C and K, as well as potassium. In addition, pomegranate seeds may promote heart health and reduce the risk of some chronic diseases.

Recommended preparation methods: Raw as a snack, in salads, as a topping for yoghurt or muesli, or as an ingredient in smoothies. Pomegranate juice can also be enjoyed, but should be consumed in moderation because of the higher sugar content.

Prickly pears

Glycemic Index (GI): 7 (very low)

Carbohydrate content: 9 g per 100 g

Fiber content: 5 g per 100 g

Protein: 0.5 g per 100 g

Fat content: 0.1 g per 100 g

Serving Size: 1 cup (about 140 g)

Glycemic load (GL): Very low

Special advantages:

- Rich in fiber, which promotes digestion and helps stabilize blood sugar levels.

- High content of vitamin C and antioxidants, which can strengthen the immune system and prevent cell damage caused by free radicals.

- Contains betalain, an antioxidant that has anti-inflammatory properties.

- May contribute to hydration due to its high water content.

Recommended preparation methods:

- Fresh, as a snack or in a fruit salad.

- In smoothies to create a creamy texture and natural sweetness.

- As an ingredient in salsas or savoury dishes for an exotic touch.

Pumpkin seeds

Glycemic Index (GI): 0 (very low)

Carbohydrate content: 14 g per 100 g

Fiber content: 6 g per 100 g

Protein: 30 g per 100 g

Fat content: 49 g per 100 g

Serving Size: 1 tablespoon (about 15 g)

Glycemic load (GL): Very low

Special benefits: Pumpkin seeds are rich in healthy fats, especially omega-6 and omega-9 fatty acids. They contain a high amount of protein, making them an excellent plant-based protein source. In addition, pumpkin seeds are packed with important minerals such as magnesium, zinc and iron. These seeds are also an excellent source of antioxidants, which can help reduce oxidative stress and boost the immune system. They also provide health benefits for the cardiovascular system and can help stabilize blood sugar levels.

Recommended preparation methods:

- **Raw:** As a snack straight from the package.

- **Roasted:** Roast in the oven with or without salt and other spices.

- **Salads:** Sprinkle over various salad dishes to add extra crunch and nutrients.

- **Baked goods:** Add to bread, muffins, or other baked goods.

- **Yogurt or smoothies:** Add to yogurt or smoothies for extra texture and nutrients.

Pumpkin seeds are versatile and can be easily incorporated into many different recipes, making them a convenient and nutritious addition to the diet of people with type 2 diabetes.

Purple carrots

Glycemic Index (GI): 16-20 (low)

Carbohydrate content: 9 g per 100 g

Fibre content: 3 g per 100 g

Protein: 1 g per 100 g

Fat content: 0.2 g per 100 g

Serving Size: 1 cup chopped (about 130 g)

Glycemic load (GL): Very low

Special Benefits: Purple carrots are not only rich in fiber, which can help stabilize blood sugar levels, but also contain a high concentration of anthocyanins, powerful antioxidants that possess anti-inflammatory properties. These antioxidants can help reduce the risk of chronic disease. In addition, they are a good source of vitamin A, which is important for vision and the immune system.

Recommended preparation methods:

- **Raw**: Ideal for nibbling or as a crunchy addition to salads.

- **Steamed**: Helps retain nutrients and tenderizes the carrots.

- **Fried**: Maintains flavor and nutrients.

- **Cooked**: Can be used in vegetable soups or as a side dish.

Due to their versatility, purple carrots can be easily incorporated into various dishes, making them a tasty and healthy option for people with type 2 diabetes.

Purslane

Glycemic Index (GI): 16 (low)

Carbohydrate content: 3.4 g per 100 g

Fiber content: 1.5 g per 100 g

Protein: 2.3 g per 100 g

Fat content: 0.1 g per 100 g

Serving Size: 1 cup raw (about 55 g)

Glycemic load (GL): Very low

Special advantages:

Purslane is a nutrient-rich plant that is especially beneficial for people with type 2 diabetes. It is rich in omega-3 fatty acids, which can fight inflammation and promote heart health. In addition, purslane contains high amounts of vitamins A, C and E, as well as essential minerals such as magnesium, calcium and iron.

Recommended preparation methods:

Purslane can be enjoyed raw in salads or smoothies. It's also a great addition to sandwiches and wraps. Alternatively, purslane can be lightly sautéed or cooked in soups and stews to increase the nutritional value of these dishes.

Quark (lean)

Glycemic Index (GI): Unknown (usually very low)

Carbohydrate content: 4 g per 100 g

Fiber content: 0 g per 100 g (fiber is not present in curd)

Protein: 12 g per 100 g

Fat content: 0.2 g per 100 g

Serving Size: 1 cup (about 250 g)

Glycemic Load (GL): Very low, depending on the portion size, the Glycemic Load remains low

Special benefits: Quark (lean) is an excellent source of protein, which is especially important for muscle building and satiety. It is also rich in calcium, which is important for bone health, and contains probiotic bacteria that can support gut health.

Recommended preparation methods: Can be eaten on its own, serve as a base for dips and spreads, or be used in combination with fruits, vegetables or herbs. Also ideal in muesli, on bread or as an ingredient in smoothies.

Quinoa

Glycemic Index (GI): 53 (medium)

Carbohydrate content: 21 g per 100 g (cooked)

Fiber content: 2.8 g per 100 g (cooked)

Protein: 4.4 g per 100 g (cooked)

Fat content: 1.9 g per 100 g (cooked)

Serving Size: 1 cup cooked (about 185 g)

Glycemic load (GL): Medium

Special Benefits: Quinoa is an excellent source of plant-based protein that contains all nine essential amino acids, making it a complete protein. It is rich in fiber and contains important micronutrients such as magnesium, manganese, phosphorus and folic acid. Quinoa also contains antioxidants, which can help reduce inflammation in the body.

Recommended ways to prepare quinoa: Quinoa can be cooked and served as an accompaniment to vegetables and lean meats. It is also great as a base for salads, as a filling for vegetables such as peppers, or as an ingredient in soups and stews. Quinoa can also be made into breakfast porridge and combined with fruit and nuts.

Quinoa is a particularly beneficial food for type 2 diabetics because it has a moderate glycemic index, which helps keep blood sugar levels stable. Its combination of fiber and protein promotes satiety and can reduce cravings.

Radicchio

Glycemic Index (GI): 12 (low)

Carbohydrate content: 4 g per 100 g

Fibre content: 3 g per 100 g

Protein: 1.4 g per 100 g

Fat content: 0.2 g per 100 g

Serving Size: 1 cup chopped (about 50 g)

Glycemic load (GL): Very low

Special benefits: Radicchio is rich in fiber and contains important vitamins such as vitamin K and vitamin C. It also provides antioxidants and can help improve digestion. It is also known for its anti-inflammatory properties.

Recommended ways to prepare: Radicchio can be used raw in salads, grilled, sautéed or as an addition to various dishes for a slightly bitter taste.

Radish

Glycemic Index (GI): 32 (low)

Carbohydrate content: 3.4 g per 100 g

Fibre content: 1.6 g per 100 g

Protein: 0.7 g per 100 g

Fat content: 0.1 g per 100 g

Serving Size: 1 cup sliced (about 116 g)

Glycemic load (GL): Very low

Special advantages:

Radishes are rich in vitamin C, which boosts the immune system, and contain antioxidants that can have anti-inflammatory effects. They have a very low calorie and carbohydrate content, making them an excellent choice for type 2 diabetics. In addition, the fiber contained in radishes promotes digestion and can help stabilize blood sugar levels.

Recommended preparation methods:

Radishes can be eaten raw, for example in salads or as a snack. They can also be used as an ingredient in sandwiches, wraps or on sandwiches. In addition, they can be steamed or added to soups and stews to add a crisp texture and slightly peppery flavor to meals.

Rapeseed oil

Glycemic Index (GI): 0 (no effect on blood sugar levels)

Carbohydrate content: 0 g per 100 g

Fiber content: 0 g per 100 g

Protein: 0 g per 100 g

Fat content: 100 g per 100 g

Serving Size: 1 tablespoon (about 14 g)

Glycemic load (GL): 0 (no effect on blood sugar levels)

Special advantages:

- Rich in monounsaturated fatty acids and omega-3 fatty acids

- May help lower cholesterol

- Contains vitamins E and K, which contribute to skin health and blood clotting

- antioxidant properties that can reduce inflammation in the body

Recommended preparation methods:

- Ideal for frying and baking due to its high smoke point

- Can be used in salad dressings or as a marinade

- Perfect for sautéing vegetables or meat

Hint:

Despite the many health benefits, canola oil should be used in moderation, especially on a calorie-conscious diet, as it is very high in energy.

Raspberries

Glycemic Index (GI): 32 (low)

Carbohydrate content: 12 g per 100 g

Fiber content: 6.5 g per 100 g

Protein: 1.2 g per 100 g

Fat content: 0.7 g per 100 g

Serving Size: 1 cup (about 125 g)

Glycemic Load (GL): Low

Special benefits: Raspberries are rich in fiber, vitamins C and K, and antioxidants. These berries also contain anthocyanins, which have anti-inflammatory properties and can reduce the risk of heart disease. Their high fiber density also promotes digestion and can help minimize blood sugar fluctuations, which is beneficial for diabetics.

Recommended preparation methods: Fresh as a snack, in yoghurt or muesli, in smoothies or salads, also as a topping for desserts.

Red cabbage

Glycemic Index (GI): 15 (low)

Carbohydrate content: 7 g per 100 g

Fiber content: 2.5 g per 100 g

Protein: 1.4 g per 100 g

Fat content: 0.1 g per 100 g

Serving Size: 1 cup chopped, raw (about 89 g)

Glycemic load (GL): Very low

Special advantages:

Red cabbage is rich in fiber, which promotes digestion and can stabilize blood sugar levels. It contains a high amount of vitamin C and vitamin K, which strengthens the immune system and improves bone health. Red cabbage also has phytochemicals such as anthocyanins, which have anti-inflammatory and antioxidant properties, helping to reduce oxidative stress and inflammation.

Recommended preparation methods:

Red cabbage can be prepared in a variety of ways, including raw, chopped in a salad, steamed, or lightly seared as a side dish. It is also excellent for fermentation into sauerkraut, which increases the probiotic benefits and supports intestinal health. Red cabbage can also be used as an ingredient in smoothies to boost nutrient density and add a vibrant color.

Rhubarb

Glycemic Index (GI): 15 (low)

Carbohydrate content: 4 g per 100 g

Fiber content: 1.8 g per 100 g

Protein: 0.9 g per 100 g

Fat content: 0.2 g per 100 g

Serving Size: 1 cup chopped (about 120 g)

Glycemic load (GL): Very low

Special benefits: Rhubarb is low in calories and contains a lot of vitamin K, as well as antioxidants that can help protect cells from damage. It is also rich in fiber, which aids digestion and keeps blood sugar levels stable. In addition, rhubarb has anti-inflammatory properties and can help lower cholesterol levels.

Recommended ways to prepare it: Rhubarb is often boiled or steamed and can be used in savory dishes, such as stews or sauces, as well as in sweet recipes, such as compote or rhubarb crumble. It is important that the leaves are not eaten, as they contain toxic substances.

Note: When consuming, the addition of large amounts of sugar should be avoided so as not to impair the positive influence on blood sugar levels. Instead, use alternative sweeteners or combine rhubarb with natural sweetness from other fruits.

Rocket

Glycemic Index (GI): 15 (low)

Carbohydrate content: 3.7 g per 100 g

Fibre content: 1.6 g per 100 g

Protein: 2.6 g per 100 g

Fat content: 0.7 g per 100 g

Serving Size: 1 cup (about 20 g)

Glycemic load (GL): Very low

Special benefits: Arugula is rich in vitamin K as well as phytochemicals such as glucosinolates and antioxidants, which have anti-inflammatory properties. In addition, it contains folic acid, calcium and vitamin A, which contributes to overall health promotion.

Recommended preparation methods: Arugula can be used raw in salads, as a topping for pizza, in smoothies or as an accompaniment to various dishes. Arugula is also excellent in pesto or sandwiches and gives a slightly spicy, peppery taste.

Rosemary

Glycemic Index (GI): Not applicable (almost no carbohydrates)

Carbohydrate content: 20.7 g per 100 g (only relevant as a dried herb)

Fiber content: 14.1 g per 100 g (dried)

Protein: 4.9 g per 100 g (dried)

Fat content: 5.9 g per 100 g (dried)

Serving Size: 1 tsp dried (about 1g) or some fresh sprigs (about 5g)

Glycemic load (GL): Very low

Special benefits: Rosemary is rich in antioxidants and anti-inflammatory compounds. It contains rosmarinic acid and carnosolic acid, which can help regulate blood sugar levels and have potentially antimicrobial properties. In addition, rosemary can promote digestion and support cognitive function.

Recommended preparation methods:

- **Fresh:** As a spice in salads, soups and various dishes.

- **Dried:** For pickling or seasoning meat, poultry, fish and vegetables.

- **Tea:** Brew some fresh sprigs or dried herbs for an aromatic tea.

- **Oil:** Rosemary oil can be used as a dressing for salads or to flavor food.

Rosemary is a versatile spice that offers not only flavor but also health benefits. It can be easily integrated into the daily diet and offers almost no risks for type 2 diabetics, as it does not have a negative effect on blood sugar levels.

Saffron

Glycemic Index (GI): 0 (zero)

Carbohydrate content: 0 g per 100 g

Fiber content: 0 g per 100 g

Protein: 11 g per 100 g

Fat content: 5.85 g per 100 g

Serving Size: Very small, typically around 0.5 g to 1 g per meal

Glycemic Load (GL): Very low (virtually zero due to minimal serving size)

Special advantages:

- Contains antioxidant compounds such as crocin, safranal, and picrocrocin, which may have anti-inflammatory effects.

- May help improve insulin sensitivity and regulate blood sugar.

- Has potential mood-enhancing properties that can be good for overall well-being.

Recommended preparation methods:

- Use in small quantities as a seasoning for rice dishes, soups, stews and baked goods.

- Can also be soaked in hot water and enjoyed as a drink.

Saffron must be used in very small quantities because it has a strong aroma and an intense flavor. It is one of the most expensive spices in the world, as the harvest is very labor-intensive.

Sage

Glycemic Index (GI): Not applicable (virtually no carbohydrates)

Carbohydrate content: 0.2 g per 100 g

Fiber content: 2.1 g per 100 g

Protein: 3.7 g per 100 g

Fat content: 12.8 g per 100 g

Serving Size: 1 teaspoon dried or a few fresh leaves

Glycemic load (GL): Very low

Special advantages:

- Contains antioxidants that can help regulate blood sugar levels.

- Rich in vitamins such as vitamin K and B6.

- Contains anti-inflammatory and antimicrobial compounds.

- May help improve memory and overall brain function by promoting communication between nerve cells.

-

Recommended preparation methods:

- Fresh or dried leaves can be used to flavor meat, fish, vegetables, and soups.

- Can be infused as a tea to benefit from its health benefits.

- Ideal for flavoring oils and marinades.

Salmon

Glycemic Index (GI): 0 (no effect on blood sugar levels)

Carbohydrate content: 0 g per 100 g

Fiber content: 0 g per 100 g

Protein: 20-25 g per 100 g

Fat content: 13 g per 100 g (depending on the type of salmon)

Serving Size: 100 g (approx. 1 fillet)

Glycemic load (GL): Very low

Special advantages:

- Rich in omega-3 fatty acids, which have anti-inflammatory effects and promote heart health.

- Good source of high-quality protein, which is important for muscle growth and maintenance.

- Contains vitamins such as D, B12 and minerals such as selenium.

- Omega-3 fatty acids can improve insulin sensitivity.

Recommended preparation methods:

- Grilling: Cook salmon fillets on the grill to add a smoky touch.

- Baking: Bake in the oven with a light marinade of lemon juice, herbs and olive oil.

- Steaming: Gentle preparation that preserves all nutrients.

- Pan frying: Fry in a non-stick pan with a low amount of oil.

- Smoking: Cold or hot smoked salmon as a delicacy and protein-rich snack.

Its glycemic properties and nutritional content make salmon an excellent choice for people with type 2 diabetes.

Sardines

Glycemic Index (GI): Not applicable (low)

Carbohydrate content: 0 g per 100 g

Fiber content: 0 g per 100 g

Protein: 25 g per 100 g

Fat content: 11 g per 100 g (of which about 1.5 g omega-3 fatty acids)

Serving Size: 1 can (approx. 100 g)

Glycemic Load (GL): Not Applicable (Low)

Special Benefits: Sardines are an excellent source of high-quality protein and contain healthy omega-3 fatty acids, which have anti-inflammatory properties and can help improve heart health. They are rich in vitamin D, calcium (through the edible bones), vitamin B12 and selenium. The omega-3 fatty acids it contains are especially beneficial for diabetics, as they can improve insulin sensitivity and reduce the risk of heart disease.

Recommended ways of preparation: Sardines can be consumed in salads, on wholemeal bread, as an ingredient in pasta dishes, or simply straight from the can. They can also be grilled or roasted well. Be sure to choose sardines in water or olive oil without added salt to control the sodium content.

Sauerkraut (no added sugar)

Glycemic Index (GI): Unknown (usually very low due to the low carbohydrate content)

Carbohydrate content: 4 g per 100 g

Fibre content: 2.9 g per 100 g

Protein: 1 g per 100 g

Fat content: 0.1 g per 100 g

Serving Size: 1 cup (about 150 g)

Glycemic load (GL): Very low

Special advantages:

- Sauerkraut is an excellent source of probiotics, which can promote gut health.

- It is rich in vitamin C, which helps to strengthen the immune system.

- Contains vitamin K2, which is important for bone health.

- Through the fermentation process, sauerkraut can improve nutrient absorption and aid digestion.

Recommended preparation methods:

- As a side dish to various main courses.

- Can be eaten raw or slightly warmed, with gentle heating preserving the probiotics.

- Also great as an ingredient in salads or as a garnish for sandwiches and wraps.

Sauerkraut is particularly suitable for type 2 diabetics because it is very low in calories, has a low glycemic load and offers numerous health benefits. Meets the needs of consumers.

Scallions

Glycemic Index (GI): 15 (low)

Carbohydrate content: 16.8 g per 100 g

Fibre content: 3 g per 100 g

Protein: 2.5 g per 100 g

Fat content: 0.1 g per 100 g

Serving Size: 1 cup chopped (about 120 g)

Glycemic load (GL): Very low

Special benefits: Shallots are rich in fiber, vitamins, especially vitamin C, and minerals such as potassium and manganese. They contain flavonoids and sulfides, which act as antioxidants and have anti-inflammatory properties. These nutrients can boost the immune system and help maintain healthy blood sugar levels.

Recommended Ways to Cook: Shallots can be used raw in salads, dressings, or salsas. They are ideal for frying, braising or roasting and add a mild, sweet onion note to dishes such as soups, sauces, stir-fries and stews.

Sesame

Glycemic Index (GI): Near zero (virtually no effect on blood sugar levels)

Carbohydrate content: 23.5 g per 100 g

Fibre content: 11.8 g per 100 g

Protein: 18 g per 100 g

Fat content: 50 g per 100 g

Serving Size: 1 tablespoon (about 9 g)

Glycemic Load (GL): Very low, especially in typical serving sizes.

Special benefits: Very rich in healthy fats (especially unsaturated fatty acids), fiber, protein, as well as important minerals such as calcium, magnesium and zinc. Sesame also contains antioxidants such as sesamin and sesamolin, which can have an anti-inflammatory effect and support heart health.

Recommended preparation methods: Can be used raw as a topping for salads and vegetable dishes, roasted for extra flavor, in the form of sesame paste (tahini) or as an ingredient in baked goods and snacks.

Type 2 diabetics can benefit from incorporating sesame into their diet, as it is a nutrient-rich option that keeps blood sugar levels stable and contributes to overall health.

Sesame oil

Glycemic Index (GI): 0 (no carbohydrates)

Carbohydrate content: 0 g per 100 g

Fiber content: 0 g per 100 g

Protein: 0 g per 100 g

Fat content: 100 g per 100 g

Serving Size: 1 tablespoon (about 13.6 g)

Glycemic load (GL): 0 (as it does not contain carbohydrates)

Special benefits: Sesame oil is rich in polyunsaturated and monounsaturated fatty acids, which can help lower LDL cholesterol and increase HDL cholesterol. It also contains important antioxidants such as sesame oil and sesamin, which may have anti-inflammatory and antimicrobial properties. It also contains vitamin E, which serves as an antioxidant and can promote skin health.

Recommended preparation methods: Sesame oil is particularly suitable for frying and frying over medium-high heat, for dressings and for refining salads and Asian dishes. It can also be used as a flavoring agent for sauces and marinades.

For people with type 2 diabetes, sesame oil can be a healthy supplement because it contains no carbohydrates and thus does not affect blood sugar. However, it should be used in moderation as it is very high in calories.

Shiitake mushrooms

Glycemic index (GI): below 20 (low)

Carbohydrate content: 7.6 g per 100 g

Fiber content: 2.5 g per 100 g

Protein: 2.2 g per 100 g

Fat content: 0.5 g per 100 g

Serving Size: 1 cup cooked (about 145 g)

Glycemic load (GL): Very low

Special benefits: Shiitake mushrooms are rich in fiber, vitamins B and D, and essential minerals such as copper and selenium. They also contain polysaccharides and lentinan, which can boost the immune system, and are known for their antioxidant and anti-inflammatory properties. Additionally, studies have shown that shiitake mushrooms can stabilize blood sugar levels and contribute to heart health.

Recommended ways to prepare: fry, steam, or use in soups and stews. They are also popular raw in salads or as an ingredient in sautéed vegetable dishes.

Soy milk (unsweetened)

Glycemic index (GI): approx. 30 (low)

Carbohydrate content: 0.5 - 1 g per 100 ml

Fibre content: 0.2 g per 100 ml

Protein: 3.3 g per 100 ml

Fat content: 1.8 g per 100 ml

Serving Size: 1 cup (about 240 ml)

Glycemic load (GL): Very low

Special advantages: Soy milk is an excellent plant-based alternative to cow's milk and has a low glycemic index, which makes it particularly suitable for type 2 diabetics. It is rich in high-quality vegetable protein and contains essential amino acids. In addition, unsweetened soy milk is low in carbohydrates, which helps keep blood sugar levels stable.

Soy milk is often fortified with vitamins and minerals such as calcium, vitamin D and B12, which are important for a balanced diet. It contains isoflavones, which have antioxidant properties and may have a positive effect on heart health.

Recommended preparation methods: Soy milk can be used in many ways. It is ideal as a base for smoothies, can be added to coffee or tea, and is a good addition to muesli or porridge. It can also be used as an ingredient in recipes for soups, sauces or baked goods to achieve a creamy consistency. Be sure to choose unsweetened varieties to avoid added sugar.

Soy sauce (low sodium)

Glycemic Index (GI): No measurable values, generally very low

Carbohydrate content: 1 g per 100 ml

Fibre content: 0 g per 100 ml

Protein: 6 g per 100 ml

Fat content: 0 g per 100 ml

Serving Size: 1 tbsp (approx. 15 ml)

Glycemic load (GL): Very low

Special advantages:

- This low-sodium version of soy sauce contains less salt, which can be especially beneficial for people with high blood pressure or other cardiovascular problems.

- Soy sauce also provides a good amount of protein and essential amino acids.

- It can enhance the taste of dishes without the need for large quantities.

Recommended preparation methods:

- As a seasoning for soups, marinades and sauces.

- To enhance vegetable dishes, especially in combination with other healthy foods such as broccoli.

- Can also be used as a dipping sauce for sushi or steamed vegetables.

Soybeans

Glycemic Index (GI): 15 (low)

Carbohydrate content: 9.9 g per 100 g

Fiber content: 6 g per 100 g

Protein: 36 g per 100 g

Fat content: 20 g per 100 g

Serving Size: 1/2 cup cooked (about 86 g)

Glycemic load (GL): Very low

Special benefits: Soybeans are an excellent source of vegetable protein, rich in polyunsaturated fatty acids, especially omega-3 fatty acids, and contain important micronutrients such as iron, magnesium, potassium, as well as vitamins of the B group. The fiber in soybeans helps improve gut health and regulate blood sugar levels. Soybeans also contain phytoestrogens, which can potentially have beneficial effects on bone health and cardiovascular health.

Recommended preparation methods: boiling, steaming, roasting, as a snack (edamame), in soups, salads or as a base for vegetable protein such as tofu and tempeh.

Spelt

Glycemic Index (GI): 45 (low)

Carbohydrate content: 70 g per 100 g

Fiber content: 10.7 g per 100 g

Protein: 14 g per 100 g

Fat content: 2.5 g per 100 g

Serving Size: 1/2 cup cooked (about 90 g)

Glycemic load (GL): Medium

Special benefits: Spelt is a nutrient-rich source of complex carbohydrates and fiber, which contributes to a slow and stable release of glucose into the blood. It contains a variety of vitamins and minerals, including manganese, phosphorus, magnesium, iron, zinc, as well as vitamins B1 (thiamine) and B3 (niacin). The fiber promotes healthy digestion and the grain has a better amino acid profile than many other types of wheat. Spelt is also less processed than traditional wheat flour, which means it contains more nutrients.

Recommended preparation methods: Spelt can be prepared in different forms such as whole grains, spelt flour or spelt pasta. It is well suited for baking bread and biscuits or as a side dish in the form of boiled grains that can be added to salads or stews. Spelt is also a nutrient-rich choice as porridge or in soups.

Spinach

Glycemic Index (GI): 15 (low)

Carbohydrate content: 3.6 g per 100 g

Fiber content: 2.2 g per 100 g

Protein: 2.9 g per 100 g

Fat content: 0.4 g per 100 g

Serving Size: 1 cup raw (about 30 g) or 1/2 cup cooked (about 90 g)

Glycemic load (GL): Very low

Special benefits: Spinach is rich in vitamins A, C, E and K, as well as folic acid, magnesium, iron and calcium. It also contains antioxidants such as lutein and zeaxanthin, which promote eye health. Spinach can reduce inflammation, lower blood pressure, and improve bone health.

Recommended ways of preparation: Raw in salads, steamed, sautéed, in smoothies or as an ingredient in various dishes such as soups, stews and casseroles.

Spring onions

Glycemic Index (GI): 10 (low)

Carbohydrate content: 7 g per 100 g

Fibre content: 2.6 g per 100 g

Protein: 1.8 g per 100 g

Fat content: 0.2 g per 100 g

Serving Size: 1 cup chopped (about 100 g)

Glycemic load (GL): Very low

Special benefits: Spring onions contain vitamin K, vitamin C, and folic acid. They are also rich in antioxidants such as quercetin, which may possess anti-inflammatory properties.

Recommended preparation methods: Spring onions can be used raw as a topping on salads or soups. They also integrate well into stir-fries, omelets or steamed vegetable dishes.

Stevia (natural sweetener)

Glycemic Index (GI): 0 (no effect on blood sugar)

Carbohydrate content: 0 g per 100 g

Fiber content: 0 g per 100 g

Protein: 0 g per 100 g

Fat content: 0 g per 100 g

Serving size: 1 teaspoon (approx. 0.5 g), which is about the sweetening power of 1 teaspoon sugar

Glycemic Load (GL): 0

Special advantages:

- **No calories:** Stevia contains no calories, making it an excellent choice for people who want or need to control their weight.

- **No effect on blood sugar:** Since stevia contains no carbohydrates and has a GI of 0, it does not affect blood sugar levels, making it ideal for diabetics.

- **Tooth-friendly:** Unlike sugar, stevia does not promote tooth erosion or tooth decay.

- **Free from artificial ingredients:** Stevia is a natural sweetener derived from the leaves of the stevia plant and contains no artificial chemical additives.

Recommended preparation methods:

- **As a sweetener for beverages:** Can be used in coffee, tea, smoothies and other beverages.

- **In cooking and baking:** Stevia can replace sugar in many recipes. However, it should be noted that stevia is much sweeter than sugar, so it should be used in much smaller amounts.

- **In desserts and yogurt:** Ideal for sweetening without added sugar.

Due to its many health-promoting properties and the fact that it has no effect on blood sugar, stevia is a popular choice for people with type 2 diabetes.

Strawberries

Glycemic Index (GI): 41 (low)

Carbohydrate content: 7.7 g per 100 g

Fibre content: 2 g per 100 g

Protein: 0.8 g per 100 g

Fat content: 0.3 g per 100 g

Serving Size: 1 cup (about 150 g)

Glycemic Load (GL): Low

Special benefits: Strawberries are rich in vitamin C, folic acid and antioxidants, which can help reduce oxidative stress. They contain polyphenols, which can have positive effects on blood sugar control. They are also low in calories and can help control weight.

Recommended preparation methods: Eaten fresh, in salads, smoothies, as a topping for yogurt or oatmeal, and in homemade desserts without added sugar.

Sugar peas

Glycemic Index (GI): 22 (low)

Carbohydrate content: 14 g per 100 g

Fiber content: 5 g per 100 g

Protein: 3 g per 100 g

Fat content: 0.4 g per 100 g

Serving Size: 1 cup raw (about 160 g)

Glycemic Load (G): Low

Special benefits: Rich in fiber and protein, contains vitamins A, C and K, as well as important minerals such as iron and calcium. In addition to a low GI and GL, the fiber in sugar snap peas helps stabilize blood sugar levels.

Recommended preparation methods: Raw as a snack or in salads, steamed or cooked as a side dish or in soups and stews.

Sunflower

Glycemic Index (GI): 35 (low-medium)

Carbohydrate content: 20 g per 100 g

Fibre content: 8.6 g per 100 g

Protein: 21 g per 100 g

Fat content: 51 g per 100 g

Serving Size: 1/4 cup (about 35 g)

Glycemic Load (GL): Low-medium

Special benefits: Sunflower seeds are rich in healthy fats, proteins, and fiber, which can help you feel full and stabilize blood sugar levels. They also contain vitamin E, magnesium and phytosterols, which are known to prevent cardiovascular disease and strengthen the immune system. The antioxidants it contains help minimize cellular damage and reduce inflammation in the body.

Recommended ways of preparation: Sunflower seeds can be eaten raw, roasted, or used in various dishes such as salads, cereals, or yogurts. They are also great as a snack or as an ingredient in homemade bread and pastry recipes.

Tahini (sesame paste)

Glycemic Index (GI): 40 (low)

Carbohydrate content: 20 g per 100 g

Fibre content: 9.3 g per 100 g

Protein: 17 g per 100 g

Fat content: 53 g per 100 g

Serving Size: 1 tablespoon (about 15 g)

Glycemic Load (GL): Low to moderate, depending on serving size

Special benefits: Tahini is rich in healthy fats, especially monounsaturated and polyunsaturated fatty acids. It also provides a good amount of fiber, which can help keep blood sugar levels stable. In addition, it is an excellent source of vegetable protein and contains important minerals such as calcium, magnesium and iron.

Recommended Preparation Methods: Tahini can be used as an ingredient in dressings, marinades, hummus or as a spread. It is also great in smoothies or as a topping for vegetable dishes.

Please note: Due to its high fat content and calorie density, tahini should be enjoyed in moderation, especially if there is a need to pay attention to the total fat in the diet.

Tangerines

Glycemic Index (GI): 47 (medium)

Carbohydrate content: 13 g per 100 g

Fiber content: 1.8 g per 100 g

Protein: 0.8 g per 100 g

Fat content: 0.3 g per 100 g

Serving Size: 1 medium tangerine (approx. 88 g)

Glycemic Load (GL): Medium to Low

Special benefits: Tangerines are rich in vitamin C, contain flavonoids and other antioxidants that can strengthen the immune system and have an anti-inflammatory effect. They also provide a moderate amount of fiber, which can aid digestion and help stabilize blood sugar levels.

Recommended ways of preparation: Can be eaten raw, ideal as a snack or in fruit salads. Tangerines can also be used for juices, but unprocessed fruits are more beneficial because they contain more fiber.

Tempeh

Glycemic Index (GI): 15 (low)

Carbohydrate content: 9 g per 100 g

Fibre content: 1.4 g per 100 g

Protein: 19 g per 100 g

Fat content: 11 g per 100 g

Serving Size: 100 g

Glycemic load (GL): Very low

Special benefits: Tempeh is a fermented soy product and an excellent plant-based protein source that may be beneficial for type 2 diabetics. It contains probiotic bacteria that can support gut health. In addition, tempeh is rich in vitamins and minerals such as calcium, iron, and magnesium, which can contribute to overall health.

Recommended preparation methods: Searing, grilling, steaming or using in curries and stir-fries. Tempeh can also be processed into slices or cubes and added to salads, sandwiches or wraps.

Thyme

Glycemic Index (GI): 5 (very low)

Carbohydrate content: 8 g per 100 g

Fibre content: 14 g per 100 g

Protein: 5.6 g per 100 g

Fat content: 1.7 g per 100 g

Serving Size: 1 teaspoon dried (about 1 g)

Glycemic load (GL): Very low

Special benefits: Thyme is rich in fiber and an excellent source of vitamin C, vitamin A, and iron. It also contains antioxidant compounds such as thymol, which have antimicrobial and anti-inflammatory properties. Thyme can help boost the immune system, aid digestion, and alleviate respiratory diseases.

Recommended Preparation Methods: Thyme can be used fresh or dried. It is ideal for seasoning meat, fish, vegetables, soups, stews and sauces. Fresh thyme can be used as a garnish, while dried thyme is usually cooked to release its flavors.

Tofu

Glycemic Index (GI): 15 (low)

Carbohydrate content: 2 g per 100 g

Fibre content: 0.3 g per 100 g

Protein: 8 g per 100 g

Fat content: 4.8 g per 100 g

Serving Size: 1/2 cup (about 126 g)

Glycemic load (GL): Very low

Special advantages:

- Rich in plant-based protein, which is important for muscle building

- Contains all nine essential amino acids

- Good source of iron and calcium

- Contains isoflavones, which have antioxidant properties and may potentially reduce the risk of certain cancers

- May help lower cholesterol

Recommended preparation methods:

- Fry or grill to get a crispy texture

- Baking in the oven with spices

- In soups or stews as a source of protein

- Marinated and then sautéed or used in salads

Tofu is a versatile, nutrient-dense option for people with type 2 diabetes that is both filling and healthy.

Tomatoes

Glycemic Index (GI): 15 (low)

Carbohydrate content: 3.9 g per 100 g

Fiber content: 1.2 g per 100 g

Protein: 0.9 g per 100 g

Fat content: 0.2 g per 100 g

Serving Size: 1 cup, diced (about 180 g)

Glycemic load (GL): Very low

Special benefits: Tomatoes are rich in vitamins A and C, as well as the antioxidant lycopene, which can help reduce the risk of certain cancers. They also contain potassium, which helps regulate blood pressure, and are low in calories overall, making them ideal for a calorie-conscious diet.

Recommended ways of preparation: Tomatoes can be enjoyed raw in salads, as an ingredient in chilies or soups, cooked in sauces or grilled. They fit seamlessly into many dishes and are a versatile addition to a balanced diet for diabetics.

Turkey

Glycemic Index (GI): 0 (low)

Carbohydrate content: 0 g per 100 g

Fiber content: 0 g per 100 g

Protein: 29 g per 100 g

Fat content: 1 g per 100 g (for lean pieces)

Serving Size: 1 piece fried (approx. 85 g)

Glycemic load (GL): Very low

Special advantages:

- Rich in high-quality protein, which is important for muscle building and muscle maintenance.

- Contains tryptophan, an amino acid that can improve mood and promote sleep.

- Good source of vitamins and minerals, especially B vitamins such as B6 and B12, which are important for energy production and nerve function.

- Lean turkey meat has a low fat content, making it an excellent choice for a calorie-conscious diet.

Recommended preparation methods:

- Grilling or frying without added fats

- Steaming or steaming

- Use in stews or salads

- Sliced as cold cuts for sandwiches

In conclusion, turkey meat is an excellent source of protein with a very low glycemic index, making it an ideal choice for people with type 2 diabetes. It provides essential nutrients and is versatile in preparation, making it easy to incorporate into a healthy, balanced diet.

Turkey breast

Glycemic Index (GI): 0 (low because it does not contain carbohydrates)

Carbohydrate content: 0 g per 100 g

Fiber content: 0 g per 100 g

Protein: 24 g per 100 g

Fat content: 1 g per 100 g

Serving Size: 100 g (about one medium slice)

Glycemic load (GL): Very low (0 because no carbohydrates)

Special benefits: Turkey breast is an excellent source of high-quality protein, which is essential for muscle building and repair. It contains hardly any fat and no carbohydrates, which makes it ideal for type 2 diabetics. Turkey breast also provides important vitamins and minerals, including B vitamins (such as B6 and B12) and selenium, which support metabolism and the immune system.

Recommended preparation methods: grilling, baking, roasting or steaming. Be sure to use little or no extra fat to keep the overall fat content low. Turkey breast can also be incorporated into salads or as the main source of protein in various dishes.

Turmeric

Glycemic Index (GI): Unknown (used in such small amounts that it has no significant effect on blood sugar)

Carbohydrate content: 65 g per 100 g

Fibre content: 21 g per 100 g

Protein: 8 g per 100 g

Fat content: 10 g per 100 g

Serving Size: 1 teaspoon (about 3 g)

Glycemic load (GL): Very low

Special benefits: Turmeric contains curcumin, a powerful antioxidant with anti-inflammatory properties. It can help regulate blood sugar levels and improve insulin resistance. In addition, turmeric is said to support digestion and strengthen the immune system.

Recommended preparation methods: As a condiment in curry dishes, soups, smoothies or golden milk. It can also be combined with black pepper to increase the bioavailability of curcumin.

Turmeric is a powerful spice that is only consumed in very small amounts, making it a safe and beneficial addition to a balanced diet for type 2 diabetics.

Umeboshi Plum

Glycemic Index (GI): Unknown/Not Relevant

Carbohydrate content: 9 g per 100 g

Fibre content: 2 g per 100 g

Protein: 1 g per 100 g

Fat content: 0.2 g per 100 g

Serving Size: 1 piece (approx. 10 g)

Glycemic load (GL): Very low

Special Benefits: Umeboshi plums are rich in antioxidants and have anti-inflammatory properties. They contain many minerals such as calcium, iron and phosphorus. They are known for their probiotic properties, which can aid digestion. They can also regulate the acid-base balance and have potential antibacterial and antiviral effects.

Recommended ways of preparation: Consume directly, add to rice, use in salads or as a spicy side dish in various dishes. Umeboshi pastes or sauces can be used as a condiment.

Unripe spelt grain

Glycemic Index (GI): 45 (low to medium)

Carbohydrate content: approx. 72 g per 100 g

Fibre content: approx. 9 g per 100 g

Protein: approx. 15 g per 100 g

Fat content: approx. 2.5 g per 100 g

Serving Size: 1/2 cup cooked (about 90 g)

Glycemic load (GL): Medium

Special advantages: Green spelt is a form of spelt that is harvested and roasted at an early stage of ripeness. It is rich in fiber, which can aid digestion and help regulate blood sugar levels. Green spelt also contains important vitamins and minerals such as vitamin B1, magnesium and phosphorus, which are essential for a healthy metabolism. It also provides a good source of vegetable protein and exhibits anti-inflammatory properties.

Recommended Preparation Methods: Green spelt can be cooked like rice or quinoa. It works well in savory dishes such as stews, soups, casseroles, and salads. Before cooking, green spelt should be soaked in water to reduce the cooking time. In addition to traditional dishes, green spelt can also be used in the form of green spelt flour to make bread and baked goods. Tip: Experiment with herbs and spices to enjoy the full flavor and maximize health benefits.

Vanilla

Glycemic Index (GI): Unknown (usually low as it is often used in small amounts)

Carbohydrate content: Low, practically negligible in pure form

Fiber content: Low

Protein: Low

Fat content: Low

Serving Size: Typically 1 teaspoon vanilla extract (about 4 g) or 1 vanilla bean

Glycemic Load (GL): Very low in typical use

Special benefits: Vanilla contains antioxidants and has anti-inflammatory and soothing properties. It can help regulate blood sugar levels and improve insulin sensitivity. Vanilla is also rich in vanillin, a compound that can fight stomach ulcers and viruses and supports the cardiovascular system.

Recommended Preparation Methods: Vanilla is great for flavoring desserts, yogurt, smoothies, and baked goods. It can be used in the form of vanilla beans, vanilla powder or vanilla extract. Since vanilla itself contains almost no calories and carbohydrates, it does not significantly affect blood sugar when used in small amounts.

Vinegar (apple cider vinegar, balsamic vinegar, red wine vinegar)

Vinegar is a versatile food that comes in different forms such as apple cider vinegar, balsamic vinegar, and red wine vinegar.

Glycemic Index (GI): 0 (very low)

Carbohydrate content: Almost zero

Fiber content: None

Protein: Near zero

Fat content: Almost zero

Serving Size: 1 tablespoon (about 15 ml)

Glycemic load (GL): Very low

Special benefits: Vinegar can lower blood sugar levels after meals and improve insulin sensitivity by delaying carbohydrate absorption in the small intestine. It also contains acetic acid, which has antimicrobial properties and can help in the digestive process.

Recommended preparation methods: Vinegar can be used in many ways, for example as a dressing in salads, as a marinade for meat and vegetables or to season dishes. Apple cider vinegar can also be diluted in water and consumed as a drink. Pasta dishes, sauces, and even desserts can be enhanced by adding balsamic vinegar, while red wine vinegar is often used in vinaigrettes and marinades.

Wakame (seaweed)

Glycemic Index (GI): Below 15 (very low)

Carbohydrate content: 9.14 g per 100 g

Fibre content: 0.5 g per 100 g

Protein: 3 g per 100 g

Fat content: 0.5 g per 100 g

Serving Size: 1 cup cooked (about 80 g)

Glycemic load (GL): Very low

Special benefits: Wakame is an excellent source of minerals such as calcium, magnesium and iron. It also contains iodine, which is important for healthy thyroid function, as well as a number of vitamins including vitamins A, C, E, and K. Wakame is also rich in antioxidants and may have anti-inflammatory properties.

Recommended ways to prepare it: Wakame can be used in soups, such as traditional Japanese miso soup. It can also be easily integrated into salads or served as an accompaniment to various dishes. Soaking the dried wakame in water before use is common; this makes the algae softer and easier to process.

Walnut oil

Glycemic Index (GI): Not applicable (no carbohydrates)

Carbohydrate content: 0 g per 100 g

Fiber content: 0 g per 100 g

Protein: 0 g per 100 g

Fat content: 100 g per 100 g

Serving Size: 1 tablespoon (about 13.6 g)

Glycemic Load (GL): Not applicable

Special advantages:

- Walnut oil is rich in omega-3 fatty acids, which have anti-inflammatory properties and are good for cardiovascular disease.

- It contains antioxidants such as vitamin E, which protects cells from free radicals.

- Walnut oil can help lower LDL cholesterol.

- It has anti-inflammatory properties that may be helpful in controlling inflammation associated with type 2 diabetes.

- It is a good source of polyphenols, which show antioxidant and anti-inflammatory effects.

Recommended preparation methods:

- Walnut oil is great as a dressing for salads.

- It can be used in smoothies or cold appetizers.

- Walnut oil can also be used to refine dishes after cooking, but it should not be used for frying due to its low smoke point (approx. 160 °C).

Walnuts

Glycemic Index (GI): 15 (low)

Carbohydrate content: 14 g per 100 g

Fibre content: 7 g per 100 g

Protein: 15 g per 100 g

Fat content: 65 g per 100 g

Serving Size: 30 g (about a handful)

Glycemic load (GL): Very low

Special benefits: Rich in omega-3 fatty acids, fiber, protein and antioxidants. They can help stabilize blood sugar levels and prevent heart disease.

Recommended preparation methods: Raw as a snack, chopped in salads, yogurt or cereals, ground in baked goods, or as an ingredient in savory dishes such as pesto.

Water (still or sparkling)

Glycemic Index (GI): 0 (not applicable)

Carbohydrate content: 0 g per 100 ml

Fibre content: 0 g per 100 ml

Protein: 0 g per 100 ml

Fat content: 0 g per 100 ml

Serving Size: 1 glass (approx. 250 ml)

Glycemic Load (GL): 0 (not applicable)

Special advantages: Water, whether still or sparkling, is calorie-free and contains no carbohydrates, proteins or fats. It plays a crucial role in hydrating the body, supporting kidney function, and helping to regulate and stabilize blood sugar levels. Adequate water intake is especially important for diabetics, as dehydration can negatively affect blood sugar levels.

Recommended ways to make it: Water can be enjoyed on its own or with a squeeze of lemon juice, cucumber slices, or a few mint leaves to vary the flavor without adding extra calories or sugar.

Water is an essential component of any diet and is an excellent way to keep blood sugar levels stable and support overall health, especially for type 2 diabetics.

Watermelon

Glycemic Index (GI): 72 (high)

Carbohydrate content: 8 g per 100 g

Fibre content: 0.4 g per 100 g

Protein: 0.6 g per 100 g

Fat content: 0.2 g per 100 g

Serving Size: 1 cup diced (about 152 g)

Glycemic load (GL): Medium (if consumed in moderation)

Special benefits: Watermelons are an excellent source of vitamin C, vitamin A, and various antioxidants, including lycopene, which has anti-inflammatory properties. Despite the high GI, watermelon has a medium glycemic load when consumed in moderate amounts, which still makes it a suitable option for diabetics, especially during the warm summer months when it additionally contributes to hydration.

Recommended preparation methods:

- In cubes in fruit salad

- As a fresh snack in slices

- In the form of unsweetened watermelon juice (be sure to monitor sugar and total fluid consumption)

Hint:

Due to the high glycemic index (GI), watermelon should be enjoyed in moderation to avoid blood sugar spikes. It may be helpful to eat them along with foods rich in protein or fiber to keep blood sugar levels stable.

Wheat bran

Glycemic Index (GI): 30 (low)

Carbohydrate content: 16 g per 100 g

Fibre content: 42.8 g per 100 g

Protein: 15.6 g per 100 g

Fat content: 4.2 g per 100 g

Serving Size: 1/4 cup (about 15 g)

Glycemic load (GL): Very low

Special advantages:

- Extremely high fiber content that aids digestion and stabilizes blood sugar levels.

- Rich in B group vitamins, especially vitamin B6 and folic acid.

- Contains important minerals such as magnesium, iron and zinc.

Recommended preparation methods:

- As an additive in yogurt or smoothies for extra fiber and texture.

- For baking high-fiber breads and muffins.

- As a topping for oatmeal or muesli.

Wheat germ

Glycemic Index (GI): 15 (low)

Carbohydrate content: 51 g per 100 g

Fibre content: 13 g per 100 g

Protein: 27 g per 100 g

Fat content: 10 g per 100 g

Serving Size: 2 tablespoons (about 14 g)

Glycemic Load (GL): Low

Special benefits: Wheat germ is an excellent source of fiber and vegetable protein, as well as rich in vitamins E and B6, folic acid, magnesium and zinc. These nutrients can help regulate blood sugar levels and promote overall health. In addition, wheat germ contains useful antioxidants that can prevent cell damage.

Recommended preparation methods: Wheat germ can be stirred raw into smoothies, yoghurts or muesli. They are also suitable for sprinkling salads, baking in bread and muffins, or as an addition to warm cereal mix.

Whole wheat flour

Glycemic Index (GI): About 50-60 (medium)

Carbohydrate content: 61 g per 100 g

Fiber content: 10-12 g per 100 g

Protein: 12-15 g per 100 g

Fat content: 3-4 g per 100 g

Serving Size: 1/4 cup (about 30 g)

Glycemic Load (GL): Medium to low depending on serving size

Special benefits: Whole wheat flour is rich in fiber, vitamins (especially B vitamins such as B1, B3 and B6) and minerals (such as iron, magnesium and zinc). The high fiber content contributes to a slower rise in blood sugar levels and promotes intestinal health.

Recommended Preparation Methods: Whole wheat flour can be used in a variety of recipes as a healthier alternative to refined white flour. Ideal for bread, pancakes, muffins, pastries and much more. However, it should be noted that whole grains should be consumed in moderate amounts in diabetics to keep carbohydrate intake balanced.

Whole wheat pasta

Glycemic Index (GI): 45 (medium)

Carbohydrate content: 25 g per 100 g (cooked)

Fiber content: 7 g per 100 g (cooked)

Protein: 5 g per 100 g (cooked)

Fat content: 1.5 g per 100 g (cooked)

Serving Size: 1 cup cooked (about 140 g)

Glycemic load (GL): Medium

Special advantages:

Whole-wheat pasta is an excellent source of fiber, which can aid digestion and help with blood sugar control. They also contain more vitamins and minerals (such as iron and magnesium) compared to refined pasta. Thanks to their higher fiber content and lower glycemic index, they help keep blood sugar levels more stable and provide a long-lasting source of energy.

Recommended preparation methods:

Wholemeal pasta can be prepared in many ways. They can serve as the basis for various healthy dishes, including:

- **Cooked whole wheat pasta:** In salads or with vegetable and protein ingredients in stir-fries.

- **Scalloped dishes:** With vegetables and low-fat cheese for a nutritious casserole.

- **Soups:** As a filling and fiber-rich ingredient in vegetable soups.

Moderate cooking of the pasta "al dente" can also help to further lower the glycemic index, which is particularly beneficial for type 2 diabetics.

Wholemeal bread

Glycemic Index (GI): 50 (medium)

Carbohydrate content: 43 g per 100 g

Fibre content: 7 g per 100 g

Protein: 9 g per 100 g

Fat content: 3 g per 100 g

Serving Size: 1 slice (approx. 30-40 g)

Glycemic Load (GL): Medium to low (depending on serving size)

Special benefits: Wholemeal bread is rich in fiber and complex carbohydrates, which slow digestion and lead to a more stable blood sugar response. It also contains numerous important vitamins and minerals such as B vitamins, iron, magnesium and zinc. The fibers in wholemeal bread promote satiety and can help keep weight under control, which is beneficial for diabetics.

Recommended ways of preparation: Can be eaten toasted or untreated. Excellent as a base for sandwiches with lean protein, vegetables and healthy fats. Can also be cut into pieces and used as croutons for salads or soups.

Wholemeal spelt bread

Glycemic Index (GI): 55 (medium)

Carbohydrate content: 43 g per 100 g

Fiber content: 8 g per 100 g

Protein: 9.5 g per 100 g

Fat content: 2.5 g per 100 g

Serving Size: 1 slice (approx. 30 g)

Glycemic load (GL): Medium

Special advantages: Wholemeal spelt bread is rich in fiber, which promotes digestion and ensures a longer feeling of satiety. It also contains a variety of vitamins and minerals, such as vitamin B complex and iron. Due to its complex carbohydrates, it helps to better regulate blood sugar levels.

Recommended preparation methods: Preferably fresh from the bakery or home-baked to ensure that there are no unnecessary additives. Can serve as a base for sandwiches or be enjoyed toasted. Combine it with protein-rich toppings such as cottage cheese or lean meats to have a balanced meal.

Wholemeal spelt flour

Glycemic Index (GI): 45 (low to medium)

Carbohydrate content: 70 g per 100 g

Fibre content: 10 g per 100 g

Protein: 14 g per 100 g

Fat content: 2.5 g per 100 g

Serving Size: 1/4 cup (about 30 g)

Glycemic load (GL): Medium

Special benefits: Wholemeal spelt flour is rich in fiber and protein, which helps stabilize blood sugar levels. It also contains a variety of minerals such as iron, magnesium and zinc, as well as B vitamins, which are important for energy metabolism. The fiber promotes intestinal health and can prolong the feeling of satiety.

Recommended preparation methods: Ideal for bread, cakes, pancakes or as an ingredient in doughs and cereals. Combine with other low-GI ingredients to create a well-balanced meal for diabetics.

Wild rice

Glycemic Index (GI): 45 (low to medium)

Carbohydrate content: 21 g per 100 g

Fiber content: 1.8 g per 100 g

Protein: 4 g per 100 g

Fat content: 0.3 g per 100 g

Serving Size: 1 cup cooked (about 164 g)

Glycemic Load (GL): Low

Special benefits: Wild rice is a good source of magnesium, zinc, vitamin B6 and folate. It contains antioxidants and is richer in protein compared to white rice. The high fiber content promotes digestion and can help regulate blood sugar levels.

Recommended Preparation Methods: Wild rice can be used as an accompaniment to many main dishes, in stews and soups, or as a base for salads. It is also great for fillings or vegetarian dishes. Before cooking, wild rice should be rinsed thoroughly and then cooked in boiling water for about 45-60 minutes until it is soft but still has a slightly firm consistency.

Xylitol

Glycemic Index (GI): 7 (very low)

Carbohydrate content: 4 g per teaspoon (about 4 g)

Fiber content: Non-existent

Protein: 0 g per teaspoon

Fat content: 0 g per teaspoon

Serving Size: 1 teaspoon (about 4 g)

Glycemic load (GL): Very low

Special advantages:

- Has a very low impact on blood sugar levels, making it particularly suitable for people with type 2 diabetes.

- Contributes to oral health by being able to reduce the risk of tooth decay and plaque formation.

- Provides about 40% fewer calories than conventional sugar, which can help reduce calories in the diet.

Recommended preparation methods:

- Can be used as a direct sugar substitute in baked goods, desserts, beverages, and various recipes.

- Ideal for lower-calorie diets and for making sugar-free sweets.

Note: Xylitol should be consumed in moderation, as excessive consumption can cause gastrointestinal discomfort in some people. It should also be kept away from pets such as dogs, as it can be toxic to them.

Yam

Glycemic Index (GI): 54 (medium)

Carbohydrate content: 27 g per 100 g

Fibre content: 4.1 g per 100 g

Protein: 1.5 g per 100 g

Fat content: 0.1 g per 100 g

Serving Size: 1 cup cooked (about 136 g)

Glycemic load (GL): Medium

Special benefits: The yam is rich in fiber, which can aid digestion and help stabilize blood sugar levels. It also contains various vitamins and minerals, such as vitamin C, vitamin B6, potassium and manganese. These nutrients support the immune system, energy production, and overall health.

Recommended preparation methods: boiling, baking or steaming. The yam can also be pureed or added to various dishes such as stews and casseroles. Be careful not to use high-sugar sauces or additives to maximize the benefits for diabetics.

Yeast flakes

Glycemic Index (GI): 0 (low)

Carbohydrate content: 9 g per 100 g

Fiber content: 5 g per 100 g

Protein: 50 g per 100 g

Fat content: 4 g per 100 g

Serving Size: 2 tablespoons (about 16 g)

Glycemic load (GL): Very low

Special advantages:

Nutritional yeast is an excellent source of B vitamins, especially B12, which are often lacking in vegetarian and vegan diets. They provide a high amount of protein and fiber, which is beneficial for satiety and blood sugar control. They also contain important minerals such as zinc, magnesium and traces of iron. The antioxidants it contains can help reduce oxidative damage and strengthen the immune system.

Recommended preparation methods:

Yeast flakes can be used in a variety of ways. They are ideal as a sprinkling ingredient over salads, soups and stews or can be used in sauces, dressings and spreads. They are also a popular choice as a cheese substitute in vegan recipes, for example over pasta dishes or in a vegan cheese sauce.

Yoghurt (Greek, unsweetened)

Glycemic Index (GI): 11 (low)

Carbohydrate content: 3.6 g per 100 g

Fiber content: 0 g per 100 g

Protein: 10 g per 100 g

Fat content: 5 g per 100 g

Serving Size: 1 cup (approx. 150 g)

Glycemic load (GL): Very low

Special benefits: Rich in protein, contains probiotics that can promote gut health, as well as calcium and vitamin B12.

Recommended preparation methods: Can be enjoyed on its own or used as a base for smoothies, dips, salad dressings or as a topping for fresh fruit and nuts.

Yoghurt (natural, unsweetened, low fat)

Glycemic Index (GI): 14 (low)

Carbohydrate content: 6 g per 100 g

Fiber content: 0 g per 100 g

Protein: 10 g per 100 g

Fat content: 1.5 g per 100 g

Serving Size: 1 cup (approx. 150 g)

Glycemic load (GL): Very low

Special advantages:

- Rich in probiotics that can support gut health.

- Contains calcium and vitamin D, which are important for bone health.

- Good source of high-quality protein that helps build and maintain muscle.

- May help keep blood sugar levels stable.

Recommended preparation methods:

- Pure as a snack or breakfast.

- As a base for smoothies, mixed with fresh or frozen fruits.

- In dressings or sauces for extra creaminess and probiotics.

- Mixed with nuts and seeds for extra flavor and texture.

IMPRINT
Information according to § 5 TMG:
Markus Gohlke
c/o IP-Management #16265
Ludwig-Erhard-Str. 18
20459 Hamburg
Contact:
E-mail: elcamondobeach@gmail.com
Phone: +491751555847
Imprint: Independently published

Made in the USA
Middletown, DE
14 December 2024

67102427R00119